THE
HIGH-SOCIETY
WIFE

THE
HIGH-SOCIETY
WIFE

BY

HELEN BIANCHIN

MILLS & BOON®

To Danilo, Lucia, Angelo and Peter
for their love and support through the years

LINCOLNSHIRE
COUNTY COUNCIL

First published in Great Britain 2005
Large Print edition 2006
Harlequin Mills & Boon Limited,
Eton House, 18-24 Paradise Road,
Richmond, Surrey TW9 1SR

© Helen Bianchin 2005

ISBN 0 263 18974 0

Set in Times Roman 17½ on 19 pt.
16-0606-37552

Printed and bound in Great Britain
by Antony Rowe Ltd, Chippenham, Wiltshire

CHAPTER ONE

'SOMETHING bothers you?'

The male voice held a faintly inflected drawl, and Gianna met her husband's dark gaze across the master bedroom with equanimity.

It was a spacious room with two walk-in wardrobes with adjoining dressing-rooms, and two *en suite* bathrooms. Beautifully carved antique furniture complemented plush furnishings in muted colours of cream and pale green.

'What makes you think that?' There was no point in relaying she'd had the day from hell, and right now she'd sell her soul for a soothing session in the Jacuzzi followed by an early night.

Instead, she'd battled peak-hour traffic, arrived home late and raced upstairs to shed her tailored business suit and take a quick shower.

The thought of attending a fundraiser held in a city hotel ballroom, where she'd graciously participate in conversation, attempt to make her way through a three-course dinner, limit herself to one glass of champagne and play the *pretend* game held little appeal.

His eyes sharpened, and for a moment she thought he'd read her mind.

'Take something for that headache before we leave.'

Oh, my. 'You know this…*because*?' Her voice sounded vaguely truculent even to her own ears.

He stood tall, with the build of a warrior, well-honed muscle and sinew flexing beneath smooth olive skin, his lithe body unadorned except for black silk hipster briefs covering his tight butt.

His dark hair was damp from a recent shower, his strong facial features all angles and planes, the dark shadow beard clean-shaven.

Dark eyes held her own. 'You want to argue?'

She waited a beat. 'Not particularly.'

One eyebrow lifted in silent cynicism before he returned to the task at hand.

Franco Giancarlo was something else, Gianna reflected as she entered her *en suite* bathroom and began applying make-up.

A ruggedly attractive man in his late thirties, who commanded respect among his peers and wreaked havoc with many a feminine heart.

Something she knew only too well. He'd captured *hers* at an impossibly young age—an adoration for a teenager ten years her senior that had shifted to hero-worship with the growing years before taking the leap to love.

An entity that had made it easy for her to accept his proposal.

For the sake of the Giancarlo-Castelli conglomerate, founded by their respective grandparents during the last century. An extremely successful business temporarily put under pressure little more than three years ago by a fatal plane crash which had claimed both Franco's parents and Gianna's widowed father.

Losses on the share market had been regained when Franco assumed directorial control. Restoring shareholders' faith had taken three consecutive successful financial quarters. Yet future stability had remained in question, given Franco Giancarlo's bachelor status and Gianna Castelli's seeming lack of interest in choosing a husband.

The two widowed grandparents, matriarchalAnamaria Castelli and patriarchal Santo Giancarlo, had presented what they had considered to be the perfect solution.

What better way to take Giancarlo-Castelli into the fourth generation than with children issued from a marriage between Franco Giancarlo and Gianna Castelli?

The fact Franco and Gianna had complied, for reasons of their own, had been cause for matriarchal and patriarchal delight.

The marriage had been accorded the wedding of the year, with a list of guests who figured high on Australia's social register. Distant relatives and far-flung friends had flown in from Italy, France and America. The event had garnered television coverage and had featured in several prominent magazines.

A year down the track they remained the golden couple, their presence at various functions duly recorded and reported by the media.

In public she could play the part of adoring wife. Yet she was conscious of an invisible barrier.

Crazy, she silently chastised. She wore his ring, shared his bed, and played the role

of social hostess with the ease of long practice. *His* in every way. Except she didn't
have his heart. Or his soul.

She told herself it was *enough*. And knew
she lied.

Dammit, what was the matter with her?
Introspection wouldn't achieve a thing, and
right now she needed to fix her hair, then
dress.

Twenty minutes later she re-entered the
bedroom to find Franco waiting with indolent ease, looking every inch the wealthy
sophisticate in a black dinner suit, his black
bow tie perfectly aligned.

Her heart leapt to a quickened beat as
sensation surged through her veins. Breathe,
she commanded silently, inwardly cursing
the way her body reacted to his presence.

Did he know? In bed, without doubt. But
out of it?

She didn't want to fall prey to such acute
vulnerability. It wasn't fair.

'Beautiful,' Franco complimented her lightly, skimming her slight curves sheathed in red silk chiffon. Undoubtedly the gown was the work of a master seamstress, with its fitted bodice and spaghetti straps. The bill for which Gianna would have insisted on paying herself.

A slight intransigence which irked him. Independence was fine, up to a point. It appeased his sensibility she'd chosen to wear the diamond drop earrings he'd gifted her on their wedding anniversary.

A matching wrap completed the outfit, and she'd swept the length of her hair high into a smooth twist held fastened with a jewelled clip. A diamond pendant rested against the curved valley of her breasts.

Stiletto heels added four inches to her height, and he crossed the room, caught the subtle Hermes perfume, and offered a warm smile.

'*Grazie.*'

'For looking the part?'

The edges of his mouth lifted a little. 'That, too.'

He offered her a glass half filled with water, and two pills.

'Playing nurse?'

'Tell me you've already taken care of it and I'll discard the role.'

Gianna merely shook her head, popped the pills and swallowed them down. 'Are we ready to leave?'

Southern hemisphere summer daylight saving meant they joined the flow of city-bound traffic while the sun sank slowly towards the horizon.

'Want to talk about it?' He hadn't missed the slight edge of tension apparent, or the faint darkness clouding her expressive features.

Gianna cast him a wry glance. 'Where would you have me begin?'

'That bad?'

Her PA had called in sick, the replacement had proved hopeless, paperwork despatched via courier had been unavoidably detained, and lunch had been a half-eaten sandwich she'd discarded following a constant stream of phone calls.

'Nothing I couldn't handle.' Wasn't that what she'd been educated, trained and groomed for?

One goal...to take her rightful place in the Giancarlo-Castelli conglomerate. Yet, like Franco, she'd begun on the lower rung of the corporate ladder, learning firsthand how the business *worked* from the ground up, winning each subsequent promotion by her own merit.

Nepotism wasn't an option in either family, and no one with any *nous* could accuse her of riding on her father or grandmother's coat-tails.

Giancarlo-Castelli were generous supporters of several worthy charities, and tonight's event held prominence among Melbourne's social echelon. Children were very dear to Gianna's heart, and the terminally ill deserved maximum effort in raising funds. She would make her own sizable donation privately.

'Show-time,' she murmured as Franco brought the powerful top-of-the-range Mercedes to a halt outside the hotel's main entrance.

The spacious foyer adjacent to the grand ballroom held a large number of invited guests, mingling as they sipped champagne. Designer gowns from home and abroad, together with a king's ransom in jewellery, graced the female contingent, while the men appeared almost clones of each other in black dinner suits, white pin-pleated dress-shirts and black bow ties.

Wealthy scions of the corporate and professional world—although none, Gianna conceded, emanated quite the degree of power as the man at her side.

Beneath the sophisticated exterior lurked a latent primitive sensuality that held the promise of unleashed passion…and delivered, Gianna accorded silently, all too aware of the intimacy they shared, when it was possible for her to lose herself so completely in him that nothing, *nothing* else mattered.

Not the longed-for gift of his love, nor the unplanned delay in conceiving his child.

'Darlings! How *are* you both?'

The breathy feminine voice was familiar, and Gianna turned with a smile, exchanged the customary air-kiss, then gave a soft laugh as the stunning blonde touched light fingers to Franco's cheek.

'Shannay.'

'Ah.' Shannay's sigh held a wistful quality as Franco carried her fingers to his lips, and she offered Gianna a conspiratorial smile. 'He does that so well.'

'Doesn't he?'

The girls' friendship went back to boarding-school days and had continued through university. They shared a similar brand of humour, had been bridesmaid honours at each other's wedding, and remained in close touch.

'Tom?'

'About to join us,' Franco drawled as Shannay's husband came into view.

'My apologies. A phone call.' Tall, lean and bespectacled, Tom Fitzgibbon was a lauded heart surgeon, and one of those rare men who understood women. A widower with two young children, he'd allowed Shannay to do all the running in their relationship, only to take the wind out of her sails at the eleventh hour.

Gianna saw Shannay's eyes soften. 'A problem?'

Tom offered his wife a musing smile. 'Hopefully not.'

Together they began to circulate, greeting mutual friends, separating as they became caught up in conversation.

The society doyennes were in their element as they worked the guests, issuing verbal reminders for upcoming events and exchanging the latest gossip.

Gianna took another sip of champagne and allowed her gaze to skim the foyer. Soon staff would open the ballroom doors and begin ushering the assembled guests to their designated seats.

Franco stood at her side as he conversed with an associate, and this close she was supremely conscious of the faint muskiness of his exclusive cologne. It teased her senses and sent warmth coursing through her veins.

Acute sensitivity heightened by sensual anticipation as to how the night would end. And just how much she wanted to savour his touch, match it and become so caught up in electrifying passion that nothing else existed.

He had the skill to take her places her wildest imagination could never cover. An emotional nirvana that was wholly primitive

and disruptively sensual when she begged
for the release only he could give.

Had other women reacted with him as she
did? Oh God no, don't answer that!

Franco had made her *his* by virtue of
marriage. Albeit an arranged union ce-
mented by mutual business issues. But what
they shared in bed was special…wasn't it?

'Hungry?'

A trick question if ever there was one! A
light musing smile lifted the corners of her
mouth as she met his gaze.

'For food?'

His eyes assumed a humorous gleam.
'Naturally. Shall we go in?'

It was then she became aware numerous
guests were moving towards the now open
doors leading into ballroom.

Their designated table was well positioned, and the guests sharing it with them
needed no introduction, which made for relaxed familiarity and ease of conversation.

Muted background music provided a pleasing ambience as wine stewards moved with swift precision among the tables, taking orders for wine and champagne, while waitresses followed in their wake bearing napkin-lined baskets of bread rolls.

It was the usual *modus operandi* for large charity events, where service, fine wines and good food formed part of the ticket price.

'You're very quiet. How is the headache?'

They were in the public eye, and as Franco's wife and a representative of Giancarlo-Castelli she was expected to *shine*.

For they numbered as one of the golden couples who were seen to have everything.

She could play the part. It was one of her talents.

Gianna let the edges of her mouth curve into a warm smile. 'Almost gone.'

He lifted a hand and brushed gentle fingers down her cheek. 'Good.'

She held his gaze, and attempted to control the way her nerve-ends began to shred at his touch. It wasn't fair to feel so emotionally naked.

With a steady hand she reached for the evening's programme and skimmed its contents.

'It looks an interesting mix,' she relayed lightly. 'A singer follows the customary speeches. There's an orchestrated fashion show. A surprise mystery guest.'

At that moment the music faded and the Master of Ceremonies took the podium, welcomed the guests, gave a brief *divertissement*, then introduced the charity's chairperson. A tireless matron who devoted her life to raising money to benefit numerous terminally ill children.

There was film coverage on the large drop-down screen of the charity's achievements, with the camera panning to children

undergoing treatments in hospital, at super-
vised play. What really caught at the heart-
strings was their expressive feature. The
solemn stoicism, the smiles, the childish
laughter.

Life went on...other people's lives.

The chairperson made an impassioned
plea for guests to provide generous donations.

Waitresses delivered the starters, and
Gianna sipped her champagne, then offered
a requested opinion as to the 'in' vacation
spot of the moment.

'I thought the Caribbean, but Paul favours
trekking through Vietnam. Can you imagine?'

'Alaska?' Gianna ventured. 'For its sce-
nic beauty and the northern lights?'

'Darling,' the woman wailed. 'I want
shopping.'

Why? she wanted to ask, when one upstairs wing of the woman's home was devoted entirely to storing clothes, with a

room designated for each of the year's four seasons. Yet another room held a collection of shoes and matching bags. A veritable treasure trove of designer gear.

The singer gave a credible performance before the main course was served, and when the plates were cleared the MC announced the fashion parade.

Beautiful models, gorgeous clothes, all shown with professional panache.

One gown in particular took Gianna's interest, and she made a mental note to visit the designer's boutique.

'You'd look fabulous in the black. Franco must buy it for you. I know just the shoes to go with it. Manolo's, of course.'

Of course. Gianna gave herself a mental slap on the wrist for her facetiousness.

As waitresses delivered dessert, the MC took the podium to introduce the mystery guest.

'A young woman who has achieved international success as an actress.'

No…it couldn't be. Yet Gianna found it impossible to dispel a growing premonition.

'She has made the very generous offer to fund an all-expenses-paid holiday for three children and their families to Disneyland.'

The announcement brought a collective murmur of appreciation from the guests.

'We have had the medical team select the names of those children fit enough to travel.' He turned towards the charity's chairperson, who had stepped onto the stage with a top hat. 'I'd like one of our esteemed guests to select three names from this hat.' He paused for effect. 'Franco Giancarlo. Would you please come forward?'

A sickening feeling settled in Gianna's stomach as Franco rose to his feet, and she watched as he crossed the floor and gained the stage.

'I'd like you all to welcome our mystery guest.' The MC paused for effect. 'Famke.'

Gianna didn't know if she could continue breathing. Tension constricted her throat and momentarily left her speechless.

Famke.

There she was, making an appearance from backstage, tall, blonde, in her late twenties, and far more beautiful than any woman had a right to be.

An actress who had initially achieved success in foreign-produced films before finding fame and fortune in America.

No one recalled her surname, for it had long been discarded in the rise to stardom.

A stunningly beautiful young woman who took pleasure in seducing wealthy men, and was known to be skilfully adept at gaining extravagant gifts of jewellery from former lovers.

Five years ago Franco had been one of them, during his sojourn in New York, before his parents' accidental death had brought him back to Melbourne.

Rumour at the time had whispered Famke wanted marriage, and the relationship soured when Franco wasn't prepared to commit. Whereupon in a fit of pique Famke had seduced an LA billionaire, married him in a blaze of media coverage and produced a child.

Gianna kept her eyes riveted on Franco, desperate to gauge his reaction while a hundred questions hammered at her brain.

What was Famke doing here? Not only Melbourne, but *here*, tonight? And why go to such elaborate lengths to ensure a public face-to-face encounter with Franco?

'She's gorgeous, isn't she?' Gianna's dinner companion observed. 'I heard she's recently divorced.'

And *hunting*.

Not *any* wealthy man, Gianna concluded with sickening certainty.

Franco Giancarlo.

CHAPTER TWO

IT WAS difficult to produce a smile as Franco rose to his feet. Yet Gianna managed it with seemingly effortless ease, and joined the guests in applauding his progress to the podium.

No one could possibly guess at the pain knifing her mid-section, or the effort it took to regulate her breathing as she caught the sexual voltage Famke exuded as Franco joined her on stage.

The actress's effusive greeting was no doubt seen by most as an orchestrated act...the brush of Famke's lips to Franco's left cheek, then the other, as a familiar European gesture.

Famke's sultry laugh, the lingering trail of scarlet-lacquered nails, were like sharp daggers piercing Gianna's vulnerable heart.

Get over it, she bade herself silently. Famke is a witch, and Franco isn't playing into her game.

Not in the public arena, a devilish voice pursued. But privately?

The possibility tore at her composure and reduced it to shreds.

It said much for her social *élan* that she managed to smile, applaud, even *laugh* at the on-stage production...for the benefit of the guests, the excitement generated in favour of the three children whose names were chosen, and the television cameras.

How long did it take? With on-screen cameos of each child, the family, with commentary? Fifteen minutes...twenty?

To Gianna it felt like a lifetime as she endured witnessing Famke's touchy-feely antics on stage, the actress's sultry smile and provocative laugh as she endeavored to display a picture of remembered intimacy with the man who numbered among her previous lovers.

Was it physically possible to *burn* with resentment whilst presenting a calm and *cool* persona?

Body language was an art form, and one she'd studied to her advantage in the business and social sector. Consequently there was no visible evidence, no betraying signals that could be noted by those who might choose to observe the effect Famke's *play* might have on Franco Giancarlo's wife.

Gianna smiled with fellow guests as Franco left the podium and returned to his table. A smile she forced to reach her eyes as he resumed his seat.

'Well done, darling,' she complimented lightly, and was totally unprepared for the brush of his lips against her own, the slow sweep of his tongue.

Reassurance? A public declaration of espousal unity?

The latter, she decided as he lifted his head away from her own.

His eyes, so dark and faintly brooding...did he glimpse what she didn't want him to see? Sense it?

Doubtful. They didn't share that degree of empathy...did they?

Almost as if he guessed at her train of thought, he threaded his fingers through her own and brought them to his lips.

He was verging on overkill, and she took it to the brink by touching gentle fingers to his cheek...resisting the urge to press the tips of her pale-pink-lacquered nails *hard* against the smooth olive skin.

To any onlookers it presented a loving gesture, but the brief flaring of those dark eyes revealed he recognised her intent, caught her restraint...and the silent promise she was far from done.

She kept the smile in place and refrained from saying a word as coffee and tea were served.

There wasn't a question if Famke might circulate among the guests, but *when*...and if the actress would make a beeline for their table and Franco, or be a little more circumspect.

A tiny humourless laugh bubbled up in her throat. *Circumspection* didn't form part of Famke's *modus operandi*.

Something which became glaringly apparent within minutes as Gianna, together with the attending guests, saw the glamorous actress appear from backstage in the glare of a spotlight.

A brilliant smile, a light laugh, followed by a seemingly touching air-kiss to the crowd at the sound of more applause…and Famke stepped down onto the ballroom floor.

Admittedly her passage was interrupted. Not so her direction. However long it took…two minutes or ten…the actress's destination was never in doubt.

Act, Gianna bade herself silently. You're good at it.

All her life she'd conformed, aware how much it meant to her father to be an exemplary daughter. To excel in school, gain honours, *show* the Giancarlo-Castelli corporation she possessed the skill to climb the corporate ladder...in a manner that proved nepotism didn't enter the equation.

A gap year spent in France had provided an opportunity to tilt at windmills... something she'd refrained from—unless riding a motorcycle behind a male student at speed or visiting a few questionable nightclubs in his company counted. Besides, there had always been a shadow bodyguard in the background, ensuring she came to no harm.

'Franco.'

The feline purr made much of his name, while the sultry heat evident in the actress's gaze set Gianna's teeth on edge.

'I just wanted to thank you, darling, for joining me on stage.'

Darling. Oh, my.

Franco's smile didn't reach his eyes. 'A public request made it difficult for me to refuse.'

Was there the suggestion of a pout forming on Famke's beautifully shaped mouth?

'Fitting, don't you think?' The actress queried with a hint of teasing censure. 'Considering your known generosity to the charity?'

With a deliberate gesture Franco caught hold of Gianna's hand and threaded his fingers through her own. 'Allow me to introduce Gianna...my wife.'

Impossible Famke was unaware of his marriage. It had received international media coverage at the time.

Blue eyes chilled to resemble an arctic ice floe for a fleeting second before the actress masked their expression.

'Such an...*interesting* alliance.'

'Famke.' She kept her tone light, and only those who knew her well would have detected the slight hint of steel beneath the surface.

'We must get together.'

'For old times' sake?' Gianna queried with pseudo-politeness, aware the invitation was aimed at Franco...solo.

A faint laugh emerged from the actress's lips. 'We *do* have a history.'

'The emphasis being *history*.'

Famke arched one eyebrow. 'I so dislike territorial women.'

'Really? Surely it adds to the challenge?'

'Afraid, sweetie?'

Gianna didn't pretend to misunderstand. Lines were being drawn, and the game was about to begin. She felt Franco's fingers tighten on her own, and ignored the silent warning. 'Perhaps Franco can answer that.'

'Why? When you're doing so well on your own.' His drawled comment caused Famke's gaze to narrow.

Unity was everything. She could do *polite*. She'd had years of practice. 'The evening is winding down, and we're about to leave.'

'Can't stand the pace?'

Gianna was sorely tempted to reveal she was taking her husband home for some hot sex. Instead, she merely smiled and rose to her feet as Franco stood and bade their immediate guests 'goodnight'.

'I'm sure we'll run into each other again before long,' Famke offered silkily.

Not if she could help it, Gianna vowed silently, barely controlling the itch to slap the actress's face.

Talk about eating a man alive!

There were friends and business associates who caught their attention as they began threading their way through the ballroom, reminders of invitations exchanged and news of upcoming social events.

She was conscious of Franco's arm along the back of her waist, the light stroke of his fingers...an attempt to soothe her ruffled composure?

Was he aware how his touch affected her? In bed, without doubt. The thought of their shared intimacy caused her pulse to leap into an accelerated beat. His mouth, hands...dear heaven. Heat flowed through her veins as sensation unfurled deep inside.

She needed the physicality of their loving, to lose herself in him and believe, for a while, that he cared. More than mere affection, and their marriage, although forging an alliance between two families, surpassed *duty*.

He'd never *said* anything. Not once, even in the throes of their lovemaking, had he mentioned the *L* word. And he never lost control. Something which irked her unbearably.

'We'll look forward to seeing you Wednesday evening.'

Get with it, a tiny voice prompted, providing a memory jog...dinner party at the home of Brad and Nikki Wilson-Smythe. 'Of course,' she managed with a smile.

It was a relief to eventually gain the hotel lobby, even more so to slip into the car and lean back against the cushioned headrest as Franco eased into the flow of traffic departing the city.

Any attempt at small-talk was out, and she didn't offer so much as a word during the relatively short drive home.

Instead, she idly noted the passing scene through the windscreen. The bright neon lights, various vehicles, the dark indigo night sky, the sturdy leafed trees lining the main thoroughfare, an electric tram...the light sprinkling shower of rain that wet the bitumen and set the windscreen wipers in action. The changing cityscape as they reached the established suburb of Toorak, with its stately homes partially hidden behind high walls and security gates.

An almost inaudible sigh whispered from her lips as Franco eased the Mercedes into their driveway.

Strategically placed lights outlined the gentle curve lined with topiary that led to the elegant two-storeyed home Franco had purchased on his return from the States.

He'd employed contractors to preserve the main Georgian-style structure, whilst completely renewing thc interior to resemble the original. Refurbishment, beautiful antique furniture, original art gracing the walls, had made it one of the most admired homes in the district, receiving media attention when he'd acquired the adjoining property, razed the existing home and added a swimming pool and tennis court.

Franco brought the Mercedes to a halt inside the multi-vehicle garage, above which resided a two-bedroom apartment occupied their trusted staff, by Rosa and Enrico, connected to the house by an enclosed walkway shrouded from the front by shrubbery. A functional gym and studio had been cleverly constructed to fit behind the walkway between the house and garages.

Together they entered the large tiled lobby, whose focal point was an exquisite crystal chandelier and a curved double staircase leading to the upper floor.

She adored the large spacious rooms, with a splendid mix of formal and informal areas occupying the ground level, the exquisite marble tiling and huge luxurious oriental rugs, and the main and guest suites situated upstairs, superbly carpeted in aubusson and furnished with genuine antiques.

'Nothing to say?'

Gianna paused and turned towards him, aware of his ability to read her so well. Too well for her peace of mind.

'An argument in the car might have proved too much of a distraction,' she managed evenly, meeting his gaze and holding it.

One eyebrow rose in silent query, and she went for the direct approach.

'Do you intend seeing her?'

His expression didn't change, although she had the distinct impression his body stilled, and for an instant there was something unreadable in those dark eyes.

'Why would I do that?'

His soft drawl sent shivers feathering down her spine, and her chin tilted a little in defence. 'Because it's what Famke wants.'

'Your trust in me is so tenuous?'

Gianna took a moment to compose the right words. 'I won't become a figure of public ridicule.'

'You want a promise of my fidelity?'

'Only if you mean it.' She turned towards the staircase. 'Promises can be broken.' It was as good an exit line as she could come up with.

Respect, affection, friendship and sexual compatibility formed the base of their marriage. *Love* wasn't supposed to enter the equation.

Yet it had, and she was willing to go on oath that a one-sided love was hell on earth.

Gianna sensed rather than heard Franco join her as she reached the upper level, and she directed him a steady glance.

'You evaded the question.'

Together they crossed the spacious central area separating each wing and made their way towards the main suite.

Gianna entered the room ahead of him and slipped off her evening sandals…a mistake, given it merely accentuated her diminutive height.

'It shouldn't require an answer.'

Her chin lifted a fraction, and her eyes were remarkably clear. She held up one hand and began ticking off each finger. 'We're joined together in marriage, legally bound in business.' Her gaze didn't waver. 'I deserve your honesty in our private life.'

Something moved in the dark depths of his eyes. 'Have I ever been dishonest with you?'

She didn't have to weigh her answer. 'No.'

'Accept that isn't going to change.'

Reassurance? Possibly. He was no fool, and she indicated as much.

He moved close and saw the way the pulse at the base of her throat jumped to a faster beat. 'A compliment, *cara*?'

That was the thing...she wasn't his *darling*. Merely a convenient partner when she longed for more...so much more.

There were those among the social clique who imagined she had it all. The trappings of extreme wealth, a perfect job, the ultimate man... Yet she'd willingly give it up in exchange for his love.

So...*dream on*, a tiny voice taunted. It isn't going to happen.

Franco took hold of her wrists, then shaped her arms to settle on each shoulder. He lowered his head and sought her lips with his own, nibbling a little, teasing until he sensed her breath catch.

She nipped at his lower lip with her teeth, held on for a few seconds, then eased back. 'What do you think you're doing?'

Stupid question. She knew exactly what he was doing!

His mouth captured hers, seeking, exploring, and wreaking havoc with her emotions as heat coursed through her veins, bringing her alive as only *he* could.

Gianna felt the familiar swirling sensation begin deep inside, and she was scarcely aware of his fingers easing the spaghetti straps of her gown aside, or the zip fastening easing open…until the red chiffon slithered to a silken heap at her feet.

Lacy red bikini briefs were all that separated her from total nudity, and her body shook a little as he traced the lace, following its pattern with a deliberate finger before easing in to stroke the soft hair curling at the apex of her thighs.

Acute sensuality arrowed through her body, and she sought the buttons on his shirt, wanting, *needing* the sensation of skin to skin, to feel and savour his warmth and essence.

'You're wearing too many clothes.' Was that husky voice her own?

He trailed a path down to her breasts and savoured one dusky peak until she groaned out loud.

'Remove them.'

How had she not noticed he'd already shrugged out of his jacket, torn off his bow tie and toed off his shoes?

Because she lost all her senses when he kissed her...except one. *Sensuality* to a heightened degree...invasive and all-encompassing.

Franco had the power to make her forget who she was, her surroundings. Everything.

There was only him, his warm musky male scent, the magic of his touch...the heat, the passion, and the wild erotic sorcery he was able to weave with her emotions.

She barely registered her fingers slipping free the buttons on his shirt, nor did she make a teasing play to draw out the moment, or seek to provoke.

Need guided the speed with which she dispensed with his shirt, freed him of the fine tailored trousers…and sought the source of her pleasure.

His indrawn breath as she enclosed him brought a soft sensual smile to her lips, and her fingers slid slowly down to cup him, only to return to create a slow, tantalising pattern that had him grasping her bottom and lifting her high against him.

Gianna cried out as his mouth closed over her breast and suckled, teasing the tender peak with the edge of his teeth before exploring its soft curve.

It was almost more than she could bear as his fingers sought and found the aroused clitoris, caressing it until she went wild, swept high by mesmeric primitive sensation.

Just as she began to ease down, he sent her up again, closing his mouth over her own in an invasive kiss that mirrored the sexual act itself.

It wasn't *enough*, and she wrenched her mouth free and told him so, demanding more...so much more.

Franco shifted, reached for the bedcovers and tossed them aside before drawing her down onto the bed.

What followed was a feast of the senses, a long leisurely tasting that drove them both to fever pitch, and it was she who lost control as her body sang to a tune only their shared sexual chemistry could evoke.

Passion...mesmeric, electric, tempestuous. A hungry slaking of the senses driven by shameless need and primeval desire.

The feel of him entering her, the long slow thrust as he slid in deep, sent every nerve and muscle into convulsing life, and she arched up to meet him when he began to move, exulting in the wonder of two people in perfect sexual accord.

Gianna became lost, so caught up in him she was unaware of the guttural cries emerging from her throat, or the soft feline purr of satisfaction so much later as Franco gathered her in against him on the verge of sleep.

Sated, she tucked a hand against his chest and burrowed in, a soft smile curving her generous mouth as he gently traced a soothing trail down her back.

Within minutes her breathing slowed into a regular pattern and she didn't feel the light touch of his lips against her temple. Nor was she aware he lay awake for some time.

CHAPTER THREE

GIANNA drifted awake to the realisation she was alone in the large bed.

Which was probably just as well, she decided as she arched her body in a preliminary stretch…and felt the faint pull of muscles, the awareness of sensitivity deep inside.

Even *thinking* about what she'd shared with Franco through the night brought renewed heat flooding her body, and she uttered a self-deprecatory groan, checked the time, saw it was early and aimed a frustrated punch at her pillow.

It was *Saturday*, for heaven's sake, with no rush to rise and begin the day.

Yet any further sleep wasn't going to happen, and she threw back the bedcovers and made for the shower.

Breakfast comprised yoghurt and fresh fruit, which she took out on the terrace.

Early-morning sun fingered the air with warmth, tempered by a wispy breeze, and lent promise to an early summer's day.

Rosa joined her with fresh coffee, and together they conferred over the coming week's schedule. Dinner at home, with the exception of Wednesday, and Gianna gave Rosa *carte blanche* with the evening meals.

A superb cook, whose culinary talents were unfailingly lauded by Gianna and Franco's guests, Rosa ran the house like clockwork, engaging outside help whenever the need arose.

It was almost nine when Gianna ran lightly upstairs to change, choosing dress jeans and a knit singlet-top. Make-up was minimal, and she swept her hair into a loose knot, secured it with a tortoiseshell clasp, then she slid her feet into stiletto-heeled boots, collected her shoulder-bag and descended the staircase.

Franco glanced up from his laptop as she entered his study, and she watched as he hit a key, then sank back in his chair.

Black jeans and black tee-shirt lent a casual air, making it impossible to ignore the way the cotton highlighted impressive muscle and sinew.

'On your way out?'

The deep drawl curled round her nerve-ends and tugged a little.

'Retail therapy,' she responded lightly.

Leading a social existence commanded serious attention to one's wardrobe. Men could wear a dinner suit several times over. If a woman wore the same gown twice to a gala event, it was assumed she couldn't afford the price of a new one. Appearance was everything, providing a benchmark for her husband's status in the business arena.

Dress designers of high repute were very much in demand, earning veritable fortunes providing original couture, with consultations and fittings afforded only by appointment.

'Have fun.' Franco's eyes gleamed with latent humour, and she offered a wry smile.

'Pray Estella is in a good mood.' The Spanish-born seamstress possessed magic fingers when it came to fabric and thread. She was also vocal, volatile, lethal on occasion when adjusting pins…and known to dismiss clientele on the slightest whim.

'Want to eat in tonight, or dine out?'

It was no contest. 'Home. Will you tell Rosa?'

'I'll cook.'

The fact he could, and well, had long since ceased to surprise her. 'OK.'

He joined her as she reached the door, and silently she tilted her head askance.

'You forgot something.' His hands cupped her face as he laid his lips against her own, then went in deep, and she held on as he bestowed an evocative tasting that blew her mind.

How long did it last? Mere seconds?

She was incapable of saying a word when he released her, and it took effort to control the slight tremble threatening her mouth as he pressed a light thumb against her lower lip.

Damn. She didn't want to appear vulnerable. Yet he had only to touch her and she became limbless.

'Go enjoy your day.' He waited a beat. 'There's just one thing. You might want to repair your lipstick.'

Repair didn't quite cover it. She'd have to start over.

'Bite me.'

His soft chuckle stayed with her as she reversed her BMW from the garage and slid in a CD, turning up the volume as she eased through the gates and gained the street.

Estella worked out of an old-style home whose rooms had been converted into a fashionista's salon. Parking rarely presented a

problem, and Gianna greeted the reception-
ist as she entered the front lounge.

Within minutes a middle-aged flamboy-
antly dressed matron appeared at the door,
hair covered in a deep crimson headpiece
that defied description, with make-up pro-
nounced to the point of absurdity.

'You are late.'

'I'm on time,' Gianna declared politely,
and incurred a haughty look.

'You would dare argue with me?'

'Perhaps we can compromise by agreeing
our watches are not in sync?'

A raven eyebrow arched in disdain. 'My
timepiece is correct. Follow me.' Estella
swept down the hallway into the fitting
room.

'Remove your outer clothes,' the seamstress demanded. 'No talking. I do not have
the inclination for chit-chat.'

Beige, taupe, cream and ivory. Who
would have thought?

Gianna watched as Estella folded the glorious silk chiffon, pinned, tucked…all the while muttering beneath her breath.

'No one has this. The fabric, the style.' The woman swept an expressive hand high. 'Your hair. Wear it up. It will give balance.' She stood back a pace. 'Jewellery minimal. Focus the gown. Shoes taupe. Fine heels. I give you fabric sample for matching. Next fitting you bring shoes. Now change and go. Next week, same time.'

Coffee, Gianna decided as she slid her sunglasses in place and slipped in behind the wheel of her car. Hot, strong, black and sweet in one of the boutique cafés, then she'd look for shoes before heading to the hairdresser.

It was after one when she consigned several brightly emblazoned packages into the boot of her car. There were still a few things she needed to do, and it made sense to take a break for lunch.

Toorak Road hosted several upmarket café's, and she chose one, ordered a long cool drink and an open salad sandwich, leafed through one of a few complimentary newspapers while she ate...and managed not to choke as Famke's image leapt off a page.

Correction. Famke and Franco, on-stage, captured on film in a momentary embrace.

Gianna forced herself to read the small print beneath the caption...then she pushed aside her plate.

It was bad enough more than a thousand guests had witnessed Famke's deliberate act. Now the incident was accessible to the entire state. Australia-wide, if other newspapers had decided to run it.

She muttered an unladylike oath beneath her breath. The doubts, ever present beneath the surface, began to emerge, insidiously invading her emotions.

Dammit. *Love* wasn't supposed to be such a *pain*.

Spending money, *serious* money, was a woman's prerogative in times of stress. And there were those stiletto heels she'd looked at, liked, and passed over.

She could afford them. Several pairs. The whole darn shop if she felt so inclined!

With that thought in mind she picked up her bag, slung the strap over her shoulder, paid her bill, emerged out onto the pavement...and came face-to-face with Famke.

The day, which had already taken a downward turn, suddenly nosedived.

'Gianna!' The actress gave a credible act of being surprised. 'This is unexpected.'

Really? Upmarket Toorak, Saturday, shopping and personal maintenance high on any career woman's list... It wouldn't be hard to do the maths.

Which meant Famke had a purpose.

Gianna gave herself a metaphorical slap on the wrist for being cynical.

'Famke.' She could do polite civility...for now.

'Let's share coffee.'

Do you honestly think I'll fall for that? 'Thanks, but we have nothing to discuss.'

'Not even the fabricated excuse of a pressing appointment?' A perfectly shaped eyebrow formed a deliberate arch. 'Afraid to hear what I might say, darling?'

Confrontation, or a silent exit? *Verbal*, definitely!

'Enjoy the hunt, Famke.'

'Straight to the point?' There was a marked pause. 'Don't bother drawing battle lines.'

'Waste of time.'

The smile didn't reach Famke's eyes. 'I'm glad you agree, darling.'

Leave, *now*. She took a step forward, only to come to an abrupt halt as the actress placed a hand on her arm.

'Don't discount the lure of sexual chemistry.'

Gianna tried for the last word. 'Yours... or mine?'

Grrr. She badly wanted to *hit* something, except it wasn't the thing to do in public.

Instead, she made for the shoe boutique, followed the purchase with a manicure, pedicure and a facial.

Consequently it was after five when she garaged her car and gathered all her purchases together.

She made the foyer and was about to ascend the stairs when Franco appeared.

'Want some help with those?'

His musing drawl put her on the defensive. So did his close proximity. He'd shaved, showered and donned black trousers and a light chambray shirt, the sleeves folded back almost to each elbow.

'I'm fine.'

Gianna missed the faint narrowing of his eyes as he examined her expressive features. 'Come toss the salad when you're done.'

'OK.'

He watched her progress up the stairs, the slight sway of her denim-clad rear, the tightly held shoulders that owed nothing to the weight of the emblazoned carry-bags in each hand.

She was a piece of work. There was strength of character, integrity, pride...and vulnerability. A combination he found intriguing.

A glass of chilled white wine rested on the kitchen servery when Gianna entered the kitchen. She'd taken time to unpack and stow her purchases, shower, and don tailored trousers and a fashionable top before slipping her feet into heeled sandals. Her hair was caught in a loose knot atop her head, and her one concession to make-up was pink lipgloss.

Franco picked up the glass and handed it to her. 'For you.'

'Because you think I need it?'

He collected his own glass and touched its rim to her own. *'Salute.'*

She wanted to slip into the light camaraderie they shared, to enjoy the anticipation of how the night would end. To *know* she could lose herself in him and emerge whole.

Except she had to deal with the spectre of Famke intruding between them. If what he'd shared with the actress came close to what he shared with *her*.

The thought of his tightly muscled body locked with Famke in the throes of love-making almost destroyed her.

A vivid imagination was fast becoming her own worst enemy. Something she must fight to control, or she'd be lost.

Pretend, a silent voice bade. You're good at it.

A redolent aroma wafted from a small pot simmering on the cook-top, and she wrinkled her nose in appreciation. 'Marinara sauce?'

'Uh-huh. Want to choose the pasta?'

Gianna didn't hesitate. 'Fettuccine.'

With easy co-ordinated movements he extracted a packet from the pantry and forked the contents into a large pot of boiling water, adjusted the heat, then turned towards her.

'How was your day?'

You really don't want to know. Yet he saw too much and read her too well. 'Fun, until Famke appeared on the scene.'

His eyes narrowed. 'Would you care to elaborate?'

She took a sip of wine, savoured the light golden liquid, then let it slide down her throat. 'Facts, or my summation?'

'Both.'

She looked at him carefully, and gained nothing from his expression. 'I bumped into her outside a café.'

'Indeed?'

'Let's go with coincidence.' Gianna lifted a hand and tucked back a lock of hair. 'I really don't want to contemplate *design*.'

She crossed to the sink, caught up the washed salad greens and began breaking the leaves into a bowl. Only to have a hand cup her chin and lift it.

'We did this last night.' His voice was pure silk.

So they had. Except it hadn't resolved a thing.

'She's on a mission.' Wasn't that the truth? 'And determined to succeed.'

'Don't let her bother you.'

'I can handle her.' *Sure* she could... verbally. Emotionally, she didn't stand a snowflake's chance in hell.

His eyes were inscrutable as he traced her mouth with his thumb, and for a few seconds she felt as if she couldn't breathe.

Then he released her and crossed to the cook-top, leaving her to finish fixing the salad.

When it was done, she set the kitchen table, checked the garlic bread heating in the oven, grated parmesan cheese and saw Franco drain the pasta.

'This is seriously *good*.' Gianna lifted her wine glass in appreciation as she sampled the food. Simple fare eaten in a homely atmosphere provided a pleasant change from their hectic social life.

'Grazie.'

His lazy drawl made her lips twitch. *'Prego.'*

'Italian conversation to match the meal?'

'Practice,' she responded lightly. 'Or have you forgotten we're entertaining Anamaria and Santo tomorrow night?'

'The grandparents,' Franco mused. 'What do you have you in mind for Rosa to serve?'

She took a sip of wine, then twirled pasta onto her fork. 'I intend to cook.'

He caught her speculative look, and bit back his amusement. 'You're planning something ambitious?'

'Uh-huh.'

'With or without Rosa's help?'

Gianna offered a brilliant smile. 'Solo. I'll devote the day to it.'

'Which will make for an interesting evening.'

Her eyes assumed a mischievous sparkle. 'Ah, you get the drift.'

She'd taken a course during a sojourn in Rome and had learnt from the best. In another life she could have been a chef. Except the sole surviving Castelli had no future in a restaurant kitchen.

Annamaria Castelli prided herself on her culinary expertise, and had personally trained her housekeeper to serve her favourite dishes. She had an acute knowledge of taste and smell, and could, she liked to boast, sample a dish and divulge not only every ingredient, but the precise measure in any recipe.

Santo Giancarlo, on the other hand, loved to eat. If it tasted fine and didn't upset his digestion, he had no inclination to examine and dissect the ingredients.

Two grandparents who were as chalk to cheese in personalities, yet with more in common than they were prepared to admit.

Gianna forked the last of her fettuccine, followed it with a morsel of garlic bread, then finished off her wine.

'You cooked; I'll take care of the dishes,' she declared, and gathered up their plates. Leaving them for Rosa didn't enter her head.

'Coffee?'

Franco rose to his feet. 'I'll make, and take mine in the study.'

'Likewise.' She needed to check e-mails, send out a few, peruse the week's business and social diary, and decide what to prepare for Sunday evening's dinner.

With deft movements she soon restored the kitchen surfaces to their former state of gleaming cleanliness, settled for tea instead of coffee, and took it into the room she used as a study.

It was late when she closed down her laptop and went to bed.

Gianna was on the verge of sleep when she sensed Franco's presence, and she went willingly into his arms as he gathered her close.

Warm skin, hard musculature, he was intensely male, and in the darkness she could pretend *want* and *need* were one and the same as his lips nuzzled the hollow at the base of her neck.

Skilled fingers trailed her slender curves, teased and tantalised until the breath hitched in her throat.

Now…dear heaven, *now*.

His mouth covered hers in a kiss that tore her apart, and she used her teeth to nip his tongue as she wound her legs around his waist.

'Greedy, hmm?'

She didn't answer, *couldn't*, as he slid inside, filling her, and she became lost, aware only of the man, the acute sensation spiralling through her body, and deep unrestrained passion…hers.

Afterwards he rolled onto his side and drew her in against him.

CHAPTER FOUR

GIANNA rose early, showered, then dressed in cargo pants and a singlet top before joining Franco on the terrace for a leisurely breakfast.

When she was done she left him reading the Sunday newspapers while she examined the well-stocked pantry.

Anamaria vowed the culinary skills of *her* housekeeper outweighed those of Santo's housekeeper, with the honour in culinary expertise being held by Anamaria herself.

Two opposing grandparents, Gianna mused, who delighted in an ongoing game of verbal one-upmanship simply for the sheer mischief it provided each of them.

After considerable thought to a menu, Gianna settled for *bruschetta*, *risotto*, with roast chicken and salad as a main. A glazed fruit flan would suffice for dessert.

She made a list, checked the chilled wine, collected her shoulder-bag, went in search of Franco and found him in his study.

He glanced up from his laptop. 'Shopping?'

'Just a few items. What are your plans for the day?'

He sank back in his chair and indicated the laptop. 'Catching up. Want any help this afternoon?'

A faint smile teased her lips. 'You can set the table.'

'Formal, of course?'

A mischievous gleam lit her eyes. 'Oh, let's do the whole bit.' Fine linen, Baccarat crystal, Christofle flatware, floral centrepiece…she made a mental note to add flowers to her list.

'Think it'll work?'

She took in his strong features, the breadth of his shoulders beneath the casual polo shirt, and felt her stomach flip at a sudden wayward thought. What would he do if she crossed round the desk, sank onto his lap and angled her mouth to his?

Reciprocate? Be amused? Indulge her?

The heat, she knew, would be all *hers*.

She had his affection. But *love* wasn't part of the deal.

Oh, for heaven's sake...*get a grip*. 'I aim to try.'

The edges of Franco's mouth lifted a little. 'Candles?'

Anamaria would wonder at the romantic setting, surmise the reason, and ask the inevitable question. 'Overkill, definitely.'

Her failure to fall pregnant after a year wasn't an issue...*yet*, Gianna qualified as she slid into her BMW and fired the engine.

A child, she contemplated as she gained the road and headed towards the main thoroughfare. Hers, but undoubtedly *his*. Something both grandparents hoped for...and assuredly one of the main reasons for the marriage between the sole surviving grandson of Santo Giancarlo and the grand-daughter of AnaMaria Castelli.

What if it didn't happen?

Oh, for heaven's sake! She was young, healthy, and there was no immediate need to rush into parenthood.

Focus on the day, she bade herself silently as she made for the closest super-market and parked.

Fresh produce was high on her list, to-gether with a freshly baked French baguette from a nearby patisserie.

Almost an hour later she retrieved her purchases from the car, carried them into the kitchen and diligently set to work.

Gianna bypassed lunch and nibbled on the end pieces of the baguette, some cheese and fruit in between tending to dinner prep-arations.

'Everything under control?'

Gianna glanced up from stirring the sauce for the *risotto*, caught Franco's amused smile and wrinkled her nose at him. 'You want to sample?' She took a spoon, scooped up a small portion, held it to his lips...and waited for his verdict.

'Perfect.' He lifted a hand and tucked a stray lock of hair behind her ear. 'I'll tend to the table.'

He'd already changed into black tailored trousers and a white chambray shirt. A quick glance at her watch revealed she should go exchange casual gear for something more respectable.

The grandparents would arrive separately around four-thirty. They'd share a glass of wine, sample a little *biscotti*, and chat. Dinner at six-thirty, coffee at nine, after which Anamaria and Santo would depart at ten.

The pattern rarely changed, Gianna conceded as she donned black evening trousers and a white silk shirt, applied make-up, added a dab of subtle perfume, slid her feet into stilettos, and retraced her steps to the kitchen.

The dining-room, she determined minutes later, resembled perfection, and she made ready a variety of serving dishes, ran a last-minute check everything could be put on hold, then cast a glance at her watch.

Security at the front gates beeped right on time, and she entered the foyer as Franco initiated the electronic release.

Would it be Anamaria or Santo heading the arrival?

Each grandparent adhered to a strict punctuality schedule, but there was the inherent need to have an edge...

Franco indicated the video screen. 'Want to check?'

'And spoil the surprise?'

Santo, by mere seconds, purring up the driveway in his red Ferrari, Gianna determined as Franco swept the imposing double entrance doors wide. With Anamaria following a car's length behind in her conventional Bentley.

Santo laughed at Anamaria's baleful glare as they each emerged from their vehicles, then graciously indicated she should precede him indoors.

'Bah,' came out as a condemnation. 'You should be ashamed of yourself, driving that ridiculous vehicle at your age.'

'Why? When it appeals to my inner child?'

'*Child* is the operative word.'

'One day I'll persuade you to take a ride with me and change your mind.'

'The whole of Venice will need to flood before I get into that contraption.'

Gianna rolled her eyes expressively as she leant in to greet her grandmother with the customary kiss to each cheek. A similar gesture from Santo followed.

'You both look well.'

A familiar compliment which she graciously accepted as she sailed...there was no other word for it...into the formal lounge.

'Tea, Nonna?'

'*Grazie.*'

'Espresso, Santo?' He'd vetoed Nonno from the onset, relaying it made him feel old.

'Too much caffeine,' Anamaria admonished. 'You won't sleep.'

'*Vecchia*, I sleep just fine.'

'You like to be called *vecchio*?'

Old woman, old man... Five minutes in, and they were already indulging in verbal warfare.

'You want I should serve pistols instead of tea and coffee?' Dammit, she was slipping into their vernacular!

Anamaria offered a sweet smile. '*Cara*, go bring the *vecchio* his coffee. He obviously needs it.'

'Don't forget to add a splash of *grappa*.' Santo's conspiratorial grin held a devilish quality.

Anamaria didn't disappoint. 'Before dinner?'

'*Vecchia*, I begin each day with it.'

A fact Anamaria knew very well. Gianna waited for the expected pithy response, but her grandmother settled for an expressive, 'Hurumph!'

'You might do well to follow my example.'

Anamaria chose to ignore him, and turned her attention towards her granddaughter.

'Is there anything you need to tell me?'

Now, there was a loaded question if ever there was one, Gianna decided with a degree of musing cynicism. 'Franco can fill you in while I go tend to the tea and coffee.'

Passing the buck? She caught the silent query and a humorous gleam in Franco's dark eyes as she sought her escape.

Tea, coffee and conversation…talk that was partly business oriented, social, and amazingly free from the grandparents' usual argumentative banter.

Had Franco issued a warning dictum? Possibly. A superb strategist, he was immune to even the most persuasive ploy.

'Gianna will show me the gardens.' Anamaria rose to her feet, indicating Gianna should do likewise. 'When we return we'll share a little wine before dinner.'

'Some fresh air will sharpen the appetite.' Franco followed her actions and sent his grandfather a musing glance. 'Santo?'

'Why disturb him?'

Santo offered Anamaria a rakish gleam. 'My dear, it will be a pleasure to walk in the garden with you.'

Anamaria's response was a castigating, 'Fool.'

'Ah, yes. But think of the fun it provides me.'

Anamaria murmured something inaudible, and at a guess it was hardly complimentary.

The early-evening air held a cool edge, and there was a premature dullness in the slowly sinking sun which surely spelled a precursor to impending rain.

Impeccably kept garden borders displayed perennials in glorious colour, clipped shrubbery planted with immaculate precision, splendid topiary and beautiful green lawn which was a testament to Enrico and the services of a regular gardening assistant.

'The roses will make a lovely display,' Anamaria ventured. 'So, too, the gladioli.'

Gianna agreed. Plants ranked high on her grandmother's list of favourite things. It was maintaining the earth, nurturing it with food and water so the seeds could stretch and grow to perfection. The right insecticides, preferably natural products.

Anamaria's garden was something to behold, with a conservatory housing indoor plants and a greenhouse filled with exotic blooms.

While Giancarlo-Castelli represented her life's work, her garden and plants assumed a secondary interest.

Now that a marriage between Gianna and Franco had been achieved, she was impatient for the birth of a great-grandchild.

Together they examined the grounds, two women with a span of almost fifty years separating them, while grandfather and the son of his son followed at a leisurely pace.

Gianna sensed the heritage, the strong bond linking each of them together, appreciating on one level the need to preserve it.

Surely a child deserved two loving parents?

Yet who would dare to suggest a child conceived from such a marriage wouldn't be loved and adored?

As a mother, her love would be unconditional…and Franco? She had a vision of him carrying a laughing child braced high atop broad shoulders, indulging the pleasure of fatherhood.

Was it asking too much for it to be the real deal? To know *she* was the love of his life, the *only* one?

Sure, Gianna discounted. That was as likely as snow falling in summertime.

And what of Famke? The glamorous actress wasn't going to fade into the woodwork any time soon.

So get your head out of the clouds and face reality, a tiny imp chastised.

'Tell Enrico a little more mulch will work wonders.'

Gianna recovered quickly. 'I'm sure he'll be delighted with your advice.'

'It's getting cool.' Franco drew level and slid an arm along the back of her waist. 'Shall we return indoors?'

They were in the presence of the grandparents... the instigators of this marriage and all too aware it wasn't a love match. Consequently there was no need to maintain any pretence.

She gave him a measured look, and gleaned nothing from his expression.

Then the moment was lost as a fat plop of rain fell on her cheek, followed by another, and they made it inside as a vivid fork of lightning rent the skies, followed almost immediately by an ominous roll of thunder.

Dinner proved a success, the serving of each course achieved with smooth expertise.

'Rosa has outdone herself.'

Anamaria's compliment was genuine, and Santo lifted his wine goblet in a silent salute and kissed his fingers in eloquent approval. 'Everything was superb.'

Gianna watched as Franco leaned back in his seat, and she fielded his musing glance with equanimity. 'I'll fetch dessert.'

The delicious glazed fruit flan added a pleasant finishing touch to the meal, and earned appreciative praise from Santo, whose penchant for anything sweet was well known.

'Go make yourselves comfortable in the lounge while I make coffee.' The suggestion followed Santo's second serving of dessert.

'Rosa has retired for the evening?'

Gianna didn't miss a beat. 'There was no need for her to stay.'

'In that case, I'll help clear the table.' Anamaria began stacking crockery while Gianna collected the serving dishes.

'You're a guest,' she admonished with a smile, and was immediately put in her place.

'Family.' Anamaria's tone didn't brook argument.

'Leave the girl alone. She doesn't want you in her kitchen.'

Santo received a withering glare in response.

'You know nothing of the kitchen.'

'I live alone. How do you imagine meals appear on my table?'

Anamaria gave a memorable snort. 'You have a housekeeper.'

'So, too,' Santo declared, 'do you.'

Franco glanced from one to the other, and positioned himself between them. 'Let's adjourn to the lounge, shall we?'

Gianna set up the coffee-maker while she dispensed china and flatware into the dishwasher, then she set up a tray, added the carafe of aromatic coffee and walked through to the lounge in time to hear Anamaria query Franco.

'You will, of course, use whatever persuasive measures are necessary?'

She placed the tray down onto the coffee table, filled each cup and handed them out. 'Are you going to enlighten me?'

'Your pregnancy,' Anamaria said without preamble.

Gianna picked up her own cup with a steady hand, and took a sip before fixing her grandmother with a level look. 'Be assured you'll be one of the first to know when it happens.'

'I'm not getting any younger, child.'

She took a deep breath, then expelled it slowly. 'You orchestrated the marriage, and I complied, aware of the necessity for a Giancarlo-Castelli heir.' Tact and diplomacy were admirable qualities, and she possessed both.

'The conception of which is our decision,' Franco intercepted silkily.

Anamaria's expression was priceless for the few seconds it took her to recover.

'Leave it alone, *vecchia.*' Santo, damn him, sounded distinctly amused. 'You obsess too much.'

'I don't require your advice.'

'Doesn't stop me from giving it.'

Anamaria replaced her cup onto its saucer and stood to her feet. Spine straight, shoulders squared, she resembled the matriarchal epitome as she gathered up her purse. 'I must thank you for your hospitality.' Good manners won out, although her voice was singularly lacking in warmth. 'My compliments to Rosa for an excellent meal.'

Gianna joined Franco as he escorted her grandmother to her car.

'Drive carefully.' The gentle edict brought a softening in Anamaria's eyes, and she laid a gentle palm to Gianna's cheek before slipping in behind the wheel.

Santo joined them as Anamaria's car disappeared through the gates. 'Women.'

The succinct disparagement brought forth a smile. 'All women?' Gianna posed with a touch of humour. 'Or one woman in particular?'

'Anamaria Castelli needs taking down a peg or three.'

She tucked a hand beneath his elbow. 'Something you've made your mission in life, huh?'

His answering chuckle said it all.

'You're wicked.' She leaned up and brushed his cheek. 'Promise me you won't speed.'

'I'll be the model of propriety.' He crossed to the red Ferrari and maneuvered himself into the bucket seat, fired the engine, then roared down the driveway, only to ease back to a discreet purr as he gained the avenue.

Gianna momentarily closed her eyes as Franco trailed his hand between her shoulders and soothed the knot of tension there.

'Interesting evening.'

'You think?'

They gained the foyer, and his hand slid to her waist as he set the security alarm.

'Sarcasm doesn't suit you.' His drawl held a tinge of amusement, and she met his level gaze with equanimity.

'I guess I should thank you.'

'For what, specifically?'

'Rescuing me.'

His dark eyes assumed a disruptive gleam. 'What do you have in mind as a reward?'

'Absolving you from helping me restore the kitchen to Rosa's preferred state of perfection?'

His soft chuckle slid along her nerves and shredded them. 'Doesn't come close.'

'You'll probably be asleep by the time I finish up.'

He pulled her in close and laid his mouth over hers. 'Doubtful.' He let her go, and moved in the direction of his study.

Yet the bedroom was empty when she entered it, and she removed make-up, discarded her clothes in favour of an over-size cotton tee-shirt and slid between the sheets.

She must have fallen asleep, for she stirred at the touch of a hand sliding over one hip in a seeking trail to her breast, and warm lips nuzzling the vulnerable curve at the base of her neck.

It was so easy to turn in to him, to savour his warmth, the hard muscled male frame, his strength. To believe, in the darkness, the intimacy they were about to share meant more than just the slaking of desire. *His.*

In his arms she became a witching wanton, eager for his touch, the sensual nirvana he unleashed, and the shattering incandescence of primitive, almost pagan sex.

Every nerve in her body vibrated with it, and afterwards she lay spent, totally lost to him. Complete, in a way she'd never dreamed possible.

CHAPTER FIVE

TRAFFIC flow was unusually heavy and therefore slow as Gianna drove into the city, with such a build-up of vehicles it took two and sometimes three changes of lights to clear each computer-controlled intersection.

Why *Monday*, for heaven's sake?

Franco had left the house an hour earlier, preferring an early start to the working day, and would have missed the congestion.

She drummed her fingers against the steering wheel and fought against reactive thought.

Famke. How long would it take for the Dutch-born model to make her next move?

Any day *soon*. Had to be. After all, why would the long-legged blonde waste time before homing in for the figurative kill?

Gianna saw the cars in front begin to move, and sent a silent prayer to the Deity she'd clear the intersection before having to battle the next. Except no one was listening.

The morning didn't get any better, with her PA calling in sick again, and just as she thought she had a handle on the workload Franco entered her office…something he so rarely did she had the feeling the day was about to get worse.

Attired in Armani tailoring, hand-stitched Italian shoes, expensive cotton shirt and silk tie, he looked every inch the directorial executive. But it was the man himself who drew attention, for he exuded an aura of power envied and coveted by many.

Gianna examined his features, and could gain little from his expression.

'I take it this isn't a social visit?'

He withdrew a folded page of newsprint and handed it to her. 'This appeared in today's edition.'

Not an extract from the city's leading newspaper, she noted, but definitely one with a wide circulation.

She skimmed the social gossip page, honed in on the photograph of Franco and Famke, read the caption, and endeavoured to control the painful knot twisting her stomach.

Famke hadn't wasted any time.

Gianna sank back in her chair and forced herself to hold his dark gaze. 'And you thought to minimise my reaction? Spare me subsequent embarrassment?' She was on a roll. 'Offer an explanation?'

'Yes.' His voice held a dangerous silkiness she chose to ignore.

'How…' The pause was deliberate. 'Considerate of you.'

'Gianna.'

Her name emerged as a husky growl, and she had the unbidden thought he wanted to wring her slender neck.

'I don't need your protection,' she managed coolly, and felt her gaze begin to waver beneath the barely leashed anger she sensed lay beneath the surface of his control.

A muscle bunched at the edge of his jaw. 'How magnanimous of you.'

'Merely your discretion.'

She could no longer look at him, didn't *dare*, for fear he'd glimpse the emotion she fought so hard to hide. Dammit, she hadn't thought anything could hurt so much. And this was only the beginning…

Franco moved round the desk, caught hold of her chin between thumb and forefinger, and tilted it.

'For the record,' he revealed with deadly softness. 'the photograph was taken five years ago. The caption is sheer conjecture, and the article itself ignores journalistic licence and lurches close to slander.'

Control yourself, she bade silently. Don't lose it.

'You're telling me this...*because*?'

He remained silent for what seemed an age, then he brushed his thumb-pad along her lower lip and released her.

'I've already fielded a few enquiries from the media. I imagine you're next on their list.'

'And you want our stories to match? Confirm our marriage is rock-solid?' She couldn't seem to stop. 'State Famke doesn't pose a threat?' She waited a beat. 'In other words...*lie*?'

His eyes hardened. 'Are you done?'

'You have my loyalty,' she said quietly. 'Do I have yours?'

A muscle bunched at the edge of his jaw. 'You have no reason to doubt me.'

It took effort to keep her voice even. 'Thank you for bringing the article to my attention.'

The air between them was electric. Something dark moved in the depths of his eyes, then it was gone.

At that moment her cellphone beeped with an incoming text message, and she heard his husky oath as she indicated the need to read it.

She was shutting him out. Had to, otherwise she'd crumble before his eyes. And she couldn't, *wouldn't* allow that to happen.

Practice allowed her to act a required part, and she arched an eyebrow in silent query.

His eyes flared, and his features hardened as he turned towards the door.

Gianna waited a few seconds before activating the SMS, and read the text with a sense of disbelief.

Like the photo? Watch this space.

There was no name, nothing to indicate the sender's identity.

Famke? Who else would text such a cryptic message?

It bothered her for what remained of the afternoon, niggled during the drive home, and by the time she entered the grounds she was ready to do battle.

Franco's top-of-the-range Mercedes sat in its customary bay, and she drew to a halt alongside, then entered the house.

The kitchen was first, and she found the comfortably proportioned housekeeper intent on fixing dinner.

'Hi, Rosa. Everything OK?'

The housekeeper offered a warm smile. 'Sure. Special delivery package came for you. I put it on your desk.'

'Thanks.' She hadn't ordered anything. Franco? She breathed in the redolent aroma. 'Mmm. Pasta *alfredo*?'

Rosa inclined her head. 'With garlic bread and salad.'

Gianna pressed fingers to her lips in a gesture of silent gratitude, then made for the stairs.

All afternoon she'd seethed in silence, cogitating how Famke could have accessed her cellphone number. And if the actress had *hers*, then it was a given she also had Franco's number.

She took a deep steadying breath as she reached the master suite, then swung open the door...only to discover an empty room, and the sound of water running in the adjoining *en suite* bathroom.

She didn't pause, just marched straight through and pulled open the shower door.

Franco, *sans* clothes, was something else. Masculinity in its most potent form, his tall muscular body sculpted to male perfection. Powerful, virile, and infinitely dangerous.

All it took was a look, and...she closed her eyes, then opened them again to meet his musing appraisal.

Damn him, he didn't appear in the least surprised, and it irked her unbearably.

'If you want to join me,' Franco drawled, 'I suggest you get rid of the clothes.'

'As if that's going to happen any time soon.'

The heat and steam proved an isolating factor as the water spray hit the marble-tiled shower base. The fact it cascaded over his tall frame did much to diminish her composure.

Get a grip. Ignore the man, focus on why you're here.

Famke…remember?

Oh, hell, maybe this wasn't such a great idea! How could she rail at him when he stood naked, water-drenched, and far too close for comfort?

'You're getting wet.'

His indolent tone prompted her into action, and she picked up the first thing that came to hand…a plastic bottle of shampoo…and threw it at him.

Two things registered simultaneously… the warning flare in his dark eyes as he fielded it with one hand and his reaching out with the other hand to haul her into the spacious shower cubicle.

'*What do you think you're doing?*' The words emerged as a scandalised scream as the shock of water streamed over her head, soaking her hair, her clothes…and oh, Lord, her shoes!

'If you want to fight, we should be on equal terms, don't you think?'

She offered something unladylike and aimed a fist at his chest. 'I could *kill* you!' She spared a glance at her suit and groaned out loud. 'Look what you've done.'

'Provide provocation, and I won't answer for the consequences.'

He was *enjoying* this. There was amusement apparent, and she lashed out at him, only to have her wrist caught in a steel-like grip.

'No, little cat.' His husky growl touched her nerve-ends and sensation skidded through her body.

'Don't.'

It was a helpless plea he ignored as he divested her of her clothes…not easily, as she fought him every inch of the way.

Naked, she stood before him in open defiance. 'I hate you.'

'Uh-huh.' He caught up the shampoo and began lathering it into her hair, rinsed it off, and massaged conditioner with such soothing effect it was difficult not to sigh her thanks and sink in against him.

She was mad at him...wasn't she? So why in hell was she just standing there?

Because it felt so darned *good*. Was that so wrong?

Next he picked up the soap and ran it over her body, then turned her away from him and eased the kinks from her neck, her shoulders, then angled the shower spray to remove the suds.

When he was done, he placed the soap in her hand. 'Your turn.'

Return his ministrations in kind? Was he kidding? How far would she get before *soaping* him became something else?

Without hesitation she handed the soap back. 'I don't think so.'

'Afraid, *cara*?'

She tilted her chin and met the devilish gleam in those dark eyes. 'Sex in the shower doesn't interest me.'

He didn't need to say he could easily prove her wrong. All it would take was the touch of his mouth on hers, the intimate brush of his body as he drew her in...and she'd be lost.

His husky chuckle almost undid her, and Gianna stepped out from the shower cubicle, caught up a towel, wrapped it sarongwise round her slender curves, then curled another into a turban over her damp hair.

She emerged into the bedroom ahead of him, and she chose a tailored skirt and cotton top, twisted her hair into a knot atop her head, and was in the process of applying moisturiser and lipgloss when Franco joined her.

Without a word she retrieved hangers and returned to the bathroom to allow her suit to dry, then she gathered up everything else and popped them down the laundry chute. As to the shoes…hopefully, if they were dried carefully and polished, they'd remain wearable.

'Replace them.'

Franco's drawled dictum held a touch of cynicism, and she turned to face him.

'If I do, I'll hand you the bill.'

'Naturally.'

He'd pulled on jeans and a polo shirt, and he didn't look any less dangerous. There was a speculative, vaguely brooding gleam in those dark eyes, making it difficult to gauge his mood.

'There's something you wanted to discuss?'

'You mean, before you became *macho-man* and hauled me into the shower?'

The element of surprise had temporarily defused the situation. Temporary being the operative word.

'You want to take it up before or after we eat?'

'Before.'

'Famke,' he divined accurately.

Cynicism lent a dark tone to her voice. 'How did you guess?'

'She is bent on making a nuisance of herself.'

'Tell me something I don't know.'

'It's not something I can control, unless she steps over the line.'

And you think she won't?

There was nothing like the direct approach. 'Does she have your cellphone number?'

His eyes hardened fractionally. 'I didn't give it to her.'

Her stomach curled into a tight ball. 'That doesn't answer the question.'

'Yes.'

The pain intensified. 'She's contacted you?'

'Personally and via SMS.' He waited a few seconds. 'I haven't responded.'

'Do you intend to?'

'No.'

Could she trust his word? Did she have a choice?

'Is there anything else?'

Suspicion wasn't proof.

'Not right at this moment.'

Franco cupped her face between his hands. 'That's it?'

She wanted to say *Don't do this to me.* Instead, she conceded steadily, 'For now.'

'Then let's go eat, hmm?'

And make pleasant conversation, while pretending Famke didn't loom like a dark spectre between them?

She'd give it her best shot.

The pasta was superb, so too was the excellent red wine they shared with the meal.

Gianna cleared the table, set up the coffee-maker and took care of the dishes while the coffee brewed.

'I'll take this in my study,' Franco indicated as he joined her, and she did likewise.

There were personal e-mails, some business data... stuff she needed to take care of, plus running a check of her social diary.

The first thing she saw when she opened her study door was the delivery package sitting on her desk, and she placed the coffee down and examined the wrapping. The destination and date stamp were partially obliterated, and, turning it over, she discovered no sender's address.

Intrigued, she undid the taping, removed the wrapping...and discovered a slightly smaller box.

A frown creased her forehead. Was this a joke?

Two more layers followed, each time revealing a smaller box. So small it could only contain jewellery...ear-studs? A ring?

Not from Franco. It wasn't his style.

Gianna removed tissue and discovered a silk-covered box. Inside was a delicate velvet pouch, which at first sight didn't appear to hold anything.

No, wait… She extracted a small piece of paper, a picture of a wedding ring. With a diagonal line through it.

The meaning was unmistakable.

She took a deep breath, then slowly released it.

Her initial instinct was to dump it on Franco's desk and demand an explanation. Except that was presumably what Famke anticipated.

The actress's goal, after all, was to cause trouble… and what better way to achieve it than to keep the barbs constant.

OK, so she'd deal with it.

Action brought reaction…but what if she didn't react as expected?

Cool, calm and collected. She could do that.

With no hesitation she scooped the packaging together and binned it.

CHAPTER SIX

TUESDAY came and went without *mishap*…if mishap related solely to contact from the stunning actress via one form or another.

Waiting for the next strike to fall made for a fraught day, and by evening's end Gianna dismissed relief as premature.

It was a game, with Famke as the master player.

Wednesday moved the tension up a notch, and although she set her cellphone for all calls to go direct to the message bank, none of them were from the actress.

'Relax.'

Gianna spared Franco a level glance as he drew the Mercedes to a smooth halt in the semi-circular driveway outside Brad and Nikki Wilson-Smythe's elegant mansion.

'I'm perfectly relaxed.'

A contradiction, but one Franco chose not to pursue as they were greeted at the door by their hostess and led in to the lounge.

'You look gorgeous,' Nikki complimented. 'Love the necklace. A recent gift?'

OK, you can do this, Gianna determined. You're good at the social thing. Educated, groomed and prepared for it. 'Thanks.' Her smile was genuine.

She'd dressed with care, choosing a classic black dress with a scooped neckline and lace overlay, and added black stilettos. Skilfully applied make-up, her hair swept into a smooth twist, and her mirrored image revealed a sophisticated young woman. Confident, assured...

How looks could be deceiving!

With practised ease she moved at Franco's side, greeting fellow guests, offering conversation, sipped the excellent Chardonnay served by her host's hired staff, and when directed she took her designated seat at the magnificent long table set with china, crystal and gold flatware.

Nikki was too well-versed in the social mores to think of seating her guests while waiting for a late arrival.

Some of Gianna's tension began to ease.

'I see you've been the recipient of a little...' there was a delicate pause '...media exposure.'

There was inevitably one person who put common sense aside in a quest to make titillating conversation.

How would Franco handle it?

As if she needed to ask!

'Interesting.' His drawled voice held deceptive indolence. 'How the press seize a past event, attach innuendo and drag it into the present.'

'Distressing, I imagine?'

'For my wife. Yes.'

Gianna placed a hand on his and a warm smile curved her mouth. 'Darling, it's of no consequence.'

She even managed to keep the smile in place as he lifted her hand to his lips and brushed a light kiss to her palm.

The tactile gesture sent the blood fizzing through her veins, heating her body at the implied intimacy. For a few timeless seconds the guests, the room, faded as she became caught up in something she couldn't afford to analyse.

Then the moment was broken by light laughter and the buzz of conversation.

Had his action been a deliberate ploy to defuse the situation? Or a genuine attempt to ease her tension?

It would be nice to think it was the latter.

Nikki had selected a number of small-portion courses to tantalise her guests' palates. Dinner parties hosted in her home involved a celebration of the senses, with the evening's theme chosen with extreme care.

Tonight the theme was Thai, and the delicacies won praise for artistic presentation and taste.

Fine food and scintillating conversation spread over several hours and, capped by superb coffee, a pleasant evening drew to a close just before midnight.

The witching hour, Gianna perceived as the Mercedes purred through the darkened streets.

'You're very quiet.'

She turned her head and took in his profile in shadow, the strong planes, the classic outline. 'I'm all talked out.'

'Tired?'

'Yes.' He could take that any way he chose!

Yet it was she who lay awake, conversely wanting his touch long after he'd fallen asleep.

What would he do if she reached out and initiated a seduction? The thought he might still her hand, her lips, was enough to prevent any move in his direction.

So much for thinking Famke might be considering a reprieve, Gianna decided as she checked her cellphone while waiting for the traffic lights to change.

Enjoy him while you can

Just what she needed to start the day. The temptation to key in a blistering response was overwhelming, except she refused to give the actress the satisfaction.

She checked the time, and saw it had been sent the previous evening.

A further SMS followed later that afternoon, equally as telling, and Gianna muttered something unladylike beneath her breath.

Last-minute data download meant she took work home and spent the evening hours cloistered with her laptop, aware Franco was similarly occupied with international conference calls.

'Ensure you leave the office on time tonight, and have Rosa serve dinner at six.' Franco drained the last of his coffee, then shrugged into his suit jacket and collected his briefcase.

Gianna looked askance, and met his studied gaze.

'Minoche,' he enlightened succinctly.

How could she have forgotten?

For the past few days they'd been like ships that passed in the night...or it seemed that way! The constraints of work, each leaving and arriving home at different times, with bed the only time they connected.

Thank heavens it was almost the weekend.

Galerie Minoche numbered high among Gianna's list of favourite art galleries, situated in a rambling old two-storeyed home whose ground level interior had been cleverly converted and beautifully crafted to retain its originality.

Privately owned by one of the city's *grande dames*, whose flamboyant persona was legend, attendance was by invitation only, with a percentage of every sale donated to a charity devoted to assisting disadvantaged children.

The ticket price was exorbitant, given it served as an obligatory donation to the same charity, with a guest list comprising the cream of Melbourne's highest social echelon.

Elegance and style were apt descriptions for what could only be termed an *event*, Gianna mused as the validity of their invitation was checked by a security guard at the main entrance, ensuring only genuine invitees were granted admission. One of several guards employed to safeguard the premises, the artwork—and the guests...guests who were given a time-frame in which to arrive, after which the gallery went into lock-down, and at evening's end an identical time-frame was provided for the guests to leave.

Dinner suits and black bow tie were *de rigueur* for the men, while the women dressed in their finest and wore jewellery whose collective worth could feed an entire Third World country.

It was strictly *smile time*, Gianna perceived as she entered the spacious reception room, for there was Minoche, hostess supreme, poised to greet them.

A tall imposing figure, attired in one of her outrageously garish kaftans, and wearing so many gold bracelets it was a wonder her arms didn't ache from the weight of them, Minoche had so long discarded any first name it was doubtful she'd ever been gifted one.

Married one year and divorced the next, she'd become a female Croesus who appeared to live only to please herself.

Little was known about her early life, and various stories abounded as to how she'd acquired her wealth.

'Gianna. Franco.' Her well-modulated voice held a trace of an accent from her French ancestry, and was at odds with her appearance.

Something, Gianna suspected, deliberately orchestrated to foster intrigue.

'So kind of you to accept my invitation.'

As if any guest would refuse! To do so without just cause would be akin to committing social suicide.

'Please, go join the guests…and enjoy!'

The finest champagne served in crystal flutes was in abundance, and the catered canapés were to die for.

Uniformed staff proffered both at every discreet turn, and it was a known fact hired staff stood in line for the opportunity to serve at Minoche's soirées.

Familiar faces, from High Court judges to scions of the medical profession, captains of business and industry, those representing old money and new, each incredibly wealthy in their own right.

These men bought with a trained eye for capital gain, should the artist ascend from relatively unknown to legendary fame, and to indulge their wives and/or mistresses.

Professional photographers were forbidden, and no cameras were permitted.

Women dressed to impress, and racked up a small fortune in body maintenance. Social gossip included a guessing game as to who had recently undergone the latest procedure. Names of good cosmetic surgeons were exchanged...preferably those residing overseas to mask the real reason for a trip.

For Gianna, it was the art which drew her interest.

Displayed in rooms and annexes, assembled by category, the canvases encompassed the avant-garde, the exotic, even the bizarre, and varying attempts to compare with the Impressionists and the Great Masters.

Vivid slashes of colour in some, muted brushstrokes in others, they represented the mood and expression of the individual artist.

Furniture and furnishings lent an ambience which heightened the works' appeal, and owed much to Minoche, whose keen interest in art lay reflected in each room, each annexe.

No expense had been spared, and Gianna had little doubt the *objets d'art*, exquisite porcelain, jade, were priceless originals, and not merely very good copies.

'See anything you like?'

She turned at the sound of Franco's voice and viewed him carefully. 'Maybe one,' she qualified on reflection. 'The artist employs a similar brushstroke technique to that favoured by Claude Monet.' The colours, however, were a little too delicate to do the garden scene justice.

'Franco. Gianna.'

The soft feminine voice was familiar...far too familiar for Gianna's peace of mind, and one she'd never thought to hear at Galerie Minoche, given the strict invitation protocol.

'Famke.' She could do polite...for now.

The actress looked even more strikingly beautiful in a black barely-there gown that alternately clung and revealed with designer perfection.

And there, at her side, stood the reason why the stunning blonde had gained entry. Gervaise Champeliere, the son of one of Minoche's closest friends, whose family wealth went through the stratosphere.

Gianna mentally gritted her teeth.

With Gervaise at her side, Famke was guaranteed entry to any soirée in the city. Oh, why not go for broke and include the entire nation, Europe, America and the United Kingdom?

'Gervaise,' Gianna acknowledged, and allowed him to kiss her hand.

Given Gervaise and Franco were friends as well as business associates, it seemed inevitable they'd spend part of the evening together.

Something Famke had deliberately orchestrated, Gianna decided, and it provided concern for just how far the actress would go in her 'Get Franco' campaign.

Nervous anxiety was hell and damnation. It kept her awake nights and clouded her thought processes.

He was *hers*, dammit.

On reflection, Franco had always been part of her picture. Older, taller, more *physical* than any male she knew. At first she'd imagined the sensual awareness she'd experienced was simply a female/male thing, perhaps even verging close to a healthy dose of hero-worship. Then he'd disappeared out of her orbit...New York, London, Milan, returning at intervals, often with a different woman in tow.

Until the accident which had altered the structure of Giancarlo-Castelli and provided the power to change their lives.

Now he was hers, and she intended to fight to keep him. Whatever it took.

'Shall we examine the exhibits?'

Franco's smooth drawl drew the actress's swift response, together with a seductive smile that hinted at a thousand delights.

Forget *hint*, Gianna accorded wryly, and go with *promise*. Damn, the woman was good! What man wouldn't rise to the occasion…literally!

She closed her eyes, then quickly opened them again. *Get a grip.*

Watching Famke work both men was a fascinating experience. Gervaise, however, was no one's fool, and Gianna doubted he was unaware of the actress's guile.

Could she attribute to Franco the same *nous*? Or was his memory enhanced by having slept with the inimical Famke?

Although *sleep* wouldn't have been on the agenda!

Dammit. If she could, she'd walk out and take a cab home. Except good manners and social etiquette forbade such an action.

It was relatively easy to slip into social mode, to smile, make conversation and give every appearance she was enjoying herself.

If Franco noticed she was overly vivacious, he gave no sign. In public, and especially in Famke's presence, she had no recourse but to accept the touch of his hand to her waist, the occasional soothing brush of his fingers down her spine, his smile, with its latent gleam of amusement, almost as if he could read her mind, her mood, and was mildly entertained by her thought processes.

After one flute of champagne she switched to mineral water, thereby ignoring the temptation to suffer Famke's presence beneath a mind-numbing influence of alcohol.

An hour in the actress's presence was too much, and she sought temporary escape in the ladies' powder room.

It didn't last long, for just as she was about to emerge Famke walked through the door.

What now?

Verbal pistols at five paces?

Gianna stifled the bubble of hysterical laughter that rose in her throat. Unless she was mistaken, the actress was on a mission, for her features lacked polite civility.

'When will you get the message?'

Oh, my, no pretence, just shoot straight for the heart, why don't you? OK, she could play this game. Hell, she even managed to dredge up a smile. 'Step aside and let you have Franco?'

Famke's eyes took on an unnatural brilliance. 'He was always going to be mine.'

'Really?' Giana inclined her head. 'Somehow that doesn't compute, given you married someone else…and so did he.'

'You poor starry-eyed fool. You think he married you for *love*?'

Forget the verbal pistols and go with up-front personal combat!

'Of course not. It's a business deal.' She waited a beat. 'The fact he's an animal in bed is a wonderful bonus.'

The actress's mouth curved into a dangerous smile. 'I doubt you indulge in any wild fantasies.'

Gianna matched the smile. 'Depends on your definition of *wild*.'

As a parting shot it didn't work, as Famke came back with a silky threat guaranteed to send shivers down the most hardened spine.

'Watch your back, darling.'

It wasn't so much the words, but the deliberate intent that accompanied them.

A fellow guest entered the vestibule, and Gianna took the opportunity to exit with a degree of dignity.

Franco appeared deep in conversation with a colleague as she re-entered the main room. Almost as if he sensed her presence he glanced in her direction and subjected her to a searching appraisal.

Looking for battle scars?

'I see no visible signs of distress,' a male voice drawled, and she turned to find Gervaise at her side.

'An interesting observation,' she offered, and glimpsed concern in his dark gaze.

'You think?' The warmth of his smile could melt a thousand feminine hearts. 'Walk with me. Let us admire the works of art, and you shall choose one for me to buy.' He glimpsed her momentary indecision. 'Famke will zero in on Franco, who in turn will choose to rescue you from my clutches.'

'Really?'

'An action which won't please Famke at all.' Amusement lit his eyes. 'Score one for Gianna.'

'Maybe.'

'If I'm wrong, you can penalise me by insisting I double my donation to Minoche's worthy charity.'

She couldn't help the soft laughter as she tucked her hand beneath his elbow. 'You're irrepressible.'

'Ah, that's what all the women say.'

Together they moved from one annexe to another, noting comparisons, studying, and were intent in discussion when Famke's voice announced, 'There you are.'

Her feline purr set the hairs standing up on the back of Gianna's neck.

'We've been looking for you.'

Sure…and little pink pigs can fly.

Gervaise indicated the pale Monet look-alike. 'Gianna has persuaded me to purchase this painting.'

'It's adorable.' The actress lifted a hand in an expressive gesture. 'The colours, the scene. And the frame is perfect.'

Adorable applied to a baby, a kitten, a puppy. A painting might live and breathe in the eye of the artist, but the end result was an inanimate entity.

'It would make the perfect gift.'

She was good. Make that very good, Gianna accorded. The question being whether Gervaise would accept the bait.

'My mother will love it.'

Madame Champeliere owned not one but two original works by the famed Claude

Monet. She wouldn't give a look-alike wall-space. So what was Gervaise's purpose, other than gifting Minoche's favourite charity a sizable donation?

Dared she assume he wasn't going to play Famke's game?

'The canvas is one Gianna admired,' Franco drawled, and Gervaise offered him a startlingly direct glance.

'Your wife has excellent taste.'

'Yes, she does.' He placed a casual arm across her shoulders. 'You'll excuse us? It's almost time to leave.'

Famke touched a hand to the lapel of Franco's jacket, then traced the seam with her finger. 'So soon?'

Minoche, the ever-vigilant timekeeper, activated an electronic buzzer on cue, then called upon her guests to settle their purchases and donations.

Millions of dollars changed hands, receipts were generated, delivery instructions given, and the guards began politely shepherding guests towards the front entrance.

Very few lingered over-long, and Gianna reached the Mercedes as Franco deactivated the car alarm.

A faint weariness settled over her shoulders as she slid into the passenger seat. Thank heavens the weekend lay ahead, with no reason to wake early and begin a workday.

It was bliss to lean back against the headrest, and she closed her eyes for the few seconds it took Franco to slip in behind the wheel.

A light sprinkling shower dotted the windscreen and rapidly intensified as Franco negotiated traffic.

'Tired?'

'Headache.' Not entirely untrue. Famke's presence tended to have that effect on her.

'You want to dissect Famke's unexpected appearance now, or later?'

His musing drawl irked her. 'You're driving, and I might want to hit you.'

She caught his gleaming gaze and barely resisted the temptation carry out her threat. Instead she opted for silence, and didn't break it when he eased the car into the garage and cut the engine.

Indoors, she made for the stairs and entered their bedroom, aware he followed close behind her.

'Don't sulk.'

Gianna whirled to face him. 'I do not *sulk*. Ever,' she added for good measure.

Did she have any idea how magnificent she looked with the fire of temper lighting her eyes? He wanted to pull her into his arms and tame that splendid rage…as only he could.

Yet she bore a fragility that made him pause, and he shucked off his jacket, undid his tie, and began loosening the buttons on his dress-shirt.

His eyes didn't leave hers, and one eyebrow slanted as she made no move to take off her clothes.

In one fluid movement he pulled his shirt free and tugged it off, then reached for the fastening on his trousers.

'Waiting for me to undress you?'

'No.'

'Pity.'

'I don't want you to touch me tonight.' Had those words been uttered impulsively by her mouth?

He toed off his shoes, stripped his socks, and followed them with his trousers. 'Your choice.'

Gianna turned away from the sight of him. Not that it did any good at all, for his image remained indelibly imprinted in her mind.

The perfectly proportioned male body, sculpted musculature, olive skin…lethal to any female's libido, especially hers.

More than anything she needed the security he offered, the warmth of his embrace…and oh, dear God, the touch of his mouth on hers. The sex, intimacy…

Fool that she was, she'd just denied herself all that with a few words issued in a moment of stupidity.

With jerky movements she discarded her evening purse, dispensed with her stilettos and removed each ear-stud, her bracelet, then reached for the clasp on her pendant.

Her fingers shook slightly and she cursed beneath her breath as the clasp failed to release. Oh, for heaven's sake, what was wrong with the darned thing?

'Let me take care of it.'

He did, easily, then he reached for the zip fastening on her gown, dealt with it, and let the silk chiffon slip to the floor.

All she wore was a thong, and he slid his fingers beneath the silk and gently slipped it free.

'Franco...' The plea whispered from her lips as his hands curved over each shoulder.

'Hush.' Franco buried his mouth in the curve of her neck, then pulled her in, savouring the taste of her, the sweetness beneath the lingering perfume, and sought her mouth with his own in a kiss that melted her bones.

With one easy movement he swept an arm beneath her knees, slid into bed and doused the lamp.

It felt so good to be held like this, with her cheek pillowed against his chest. His heartbeat rhythm was strong beneath her ear, and she stretched an arm across his midriff, then sank in as he brushed a soothing path along her spine.

'Sleep, hmm?'

He didn't see the shimmer of tears before she stilled their fall.

She would have given anything to possess the courage to arouse him with her hands, her mouth. Pleasure him as he pleasured her and gift him anything he chose to ask.

Would he reciprocate?

The insecurity of not being able to antic- ipate his reaction, together with the possi- bility of his rejection, stayed with her long after he fell asleep.

CHAPTER SEVEN

GIANNA left the house mid-morning for a final dress fitting with Estella. The stilettos she intended to wear reposed in their shoe-box, and she'd collect material swatches to ensure the right choice of lipstick.

The charity fundraiser ball wasn't scheduled for another fortnight, but there was nothing like being prepared.

'Ah, *yes*.' Estella applauded. 'The shoes are magnificent.' Her features became stern. 'You will remember my suggestion for jewellery. And you will wear your hair up… yes?'

'Of course.'

'You intend shopping? You leave the gown here and collect on your way home. No one must see it in your car.'

Payment was made, swatches provided, and she gave the gifted seamstress an impulsive hug as she left. 'Thank you.'

'Go,' Estella bade gruffly.

The manicurist was next on Gianna's list, followed by lunch, then she spent time with a beautician, matching lipstick and eyeshadow until it was agreed the perfect blend had been achieved.

It was almost five when she arrived home, and as soon as she stowed her packages she hit the shower, pulled on jeans and a tee-shirt, then joined Franco for dinner.

'I take it you had a successful day?'

'Shopping,' Gianna enlightened him succinctly. 'It's one of women's finest sins.'

His soft laughter curled round her heart and squeezed a little.

'Should I even suggest you define other sins?'

She pretended to consider a mental list as she forked the last morsel of food from her plate. 'What else is there?'

'I can name a few.'

'Well, there's gourmet food. Belgian chocolate. Cristal champagne. Then there's pleasures of the flesh…a fabulous massage, facial, pampering time at an upmarket luxury spa.' She paused imperceptibly. 'I guess good sex deserves a place.'

Best not to tell him she placed the latter very high on her personal list of fine things. He took good sex and made it into a sensual banquet…truly a feast of the senses. A lover who ensured his woman derived the ultimate pleasure before joining her to take his own.

Gianna checked her watch. 'Time to go change.'

She cleared the table and stacked china and flatware in the dishwasher, then ran lightly upstairs.

Choosing what to wear didn't pose a problem, and Gianna selected black silk evening trousers, a matching silk camisole, and added a black velvet jacket beautifully decorated with delicately patterned gold thread. Black stilettos, exquisite gold jewellery, subtly applied make-up, and she was ready.

Franco shrugged into his suit jacket and adjusted his tie as she collected her evening purse.

His presence dominated the room, his aura of power disruptive, and he exuded a compelling sensuality that never failed to catch her breath.

Attired in Armani, shod by Magli, he was something else. No one man deserved to look the way he did.

Excellent genes. Had to be, Gianna decided as she slid into the passenger seat.

Was it any wonder he drew the eye of every woman between seventeen and seventy?

Tickets for the Cirque du Soleil held at the city's casino had sold out within days, with a review for the current show according it sensational.

Glitz and glamour ruled as they entered the large foyer, and Franco curved an arm round her waist as they made their way towards the auditorium.

Due care? An outward sign of ownership? Projecting a public image?

Oh, for heaven's sake, Gianna chided beneath her breath. Stop analysing his every action!

What was the matter with her? Since when had she become so super-sensitive?

The answer was simple. Ever since a certain tall long-legged blonde actress had burst onto the scene.

'You're very quiet.'

His indolent drawl curled round her nerve-ends and tugged a little.

'What would you like me to say?' Gianna sent him a stunning smile. 'It's a beautiful night? The show promises to be great?' *Are you spending time with Famke?*

'Can I get you a drink?'

Now, there's a thought. A flute or two of champagne and she'd float through the next few hours. 'No, thanks.'

'Something bothers you?'

Someone, she amended silently. 'What makes you think that?'

He read her too well. The too-bright smile, a tenseness that made her pulse beat a little faster.

'Shall we take our seats?'

Within minutes the lights dimmed, the curtains slid aside, and the show began.

At that moment two latecomers passed by, to occupy the two adjoining seats.

'Gianna.'

She didn't believe it. 'Shannay?'

'Franco's idea,' Shannay revealed quietly.

The evening had just become better, and she settled down to enjoy the stage presentation.

Such colour, balance and symmetry. Beauty in fluid movement and spectacle.

The highly trained performers deserved all the plaudits afforded them. The audience were enthusiastic and generous with their applause, and Gianna experienced regret when the show came to an end.

'Let's go find somewhere quiet and share a drink.' Shannay tucked a hand beneath Gianna's elbow. 'Tom's mother is staying over, so we don't need to rush back to relieve a babysitter, and—'

'My wife wants to party.'

Tom's slightly rueful expression brought a bubble of laughter as Gianna joined in the game. 'Well, then, what are we waiting for?'

'An hour.' Shannay reached up and planted a kiss on her husband's mouth. 'I promise.'

'I've booked a suite here overnight.'

Shannay turned towards Gianna. 'Let me rework that suggestion.' She gave a mischievous grin. 'Ten minutes, one drink.'

Then she swung back to embrace her husband. 'I adore you.'

'Same goes.'

Sweet pain pierced Gianna's heart at the look they exchanged. It was the stuff of wishes...the highly emotive kind, and unconditional love. Beyond price.

For a moment it made her ache for the impossible, then she banked it down, and kept a smile pinned in place.

They found a bar, Franco ordered champagne, and Gianna had barely taken a few sips when Shannay warned quietly, 'Isn't that—?'

'Franco! Who would have thought to see you here?'

'Famke,' Shannay concluded.

Gianna killed the uncharitable thought the actress seemed bent on discovering their every move. Coincidence wasn't a believable option.

'I'm with friends.' Famke outlined the lapel of Franco's jacket with a scarlet-lacquered nail. 'We'll join you.'

Not if she could help it! 'Thanks, but—'

'No thanks?' The actress offered Franco a seductive smile. 'Another time, *caro*. Hmm?' She didn't wait for an acknowledgment as she walked away.

Swayed was a more apt description, and in a perfectly timed manoeuvre, Famke paused at ten paces and took a few seconds to shoot Franco a provocative glance over one shoulder.

'Should we applaud?'

Gianna caught Shannay's quiet cynicism and rolled her eyes. 'Overkill, definitely.'

'She's a witch.'

'Dangerous.'

'And then some. We need a strategy,' Shannay declared with determination, and Gianna lifted an eyebrow.

'*We* do?'

'Uh-huh.' She leaned in close. 'I'll call you.' With that she tucked a hand through her husband's arm. 'You mentioned a suite?'

Gianna bit down a wistful smile as she watched them leave.

'Want to try your luck in the casino?'

Why not? 'OK.'

Bright lights, a heavy crowd, and noise. Fun for a while, Gianna decided as she changed cash for chips and chose the spinning wheel, won and lost, and gave up on it. Franco, on the other hand, won. Naturally.

'Had enough?'

A whoop of excitement sounded from a nearby table, and she saw the croupier push a pile of chips towards the winner.

A roll of the dice looked interesting, but first the powder room. 'Five minutes,' she indicated. 'I'll be back.'

There was an opportunity to freshen her make-up, and she'd no sooner smoothed her hair and capped her lipstick when Famke joined her at the mirrored wall above the long bench of washbasins.

The thought the actress might be on a stalking mission was slightly freaky. Ditto the startlingly blue gaze via the mirrored reflection, for the smile was absent and there was no pretence at civility apparent.

Great. Verbal sabres at midnight! Just what she needed. What was it about attack being the best form of defence?

'You have something you want to say?' Nothing like diving headfirst into deep waters.

'Franco's mine.'

Gianna arched an eyebrow. 'And I'm history?'

'Got it in one, darling.'

'If you think I'll meekly step aside... forget it.'

Famke directed a pitying look. 'Sweetheart, I can do things for him you've never even heard of.'

Oh, my. This was getting down and dirty. 'You think?'

The actress ran the tip of her tongue over the edge of her teeth. 'Without doubt.'

Time for the punchline. 'Sexual tricks, Famke? How sad you need to resort to them.'

She almost made it to the door.

'Jealous, darling?'

Gianna didn't qualify the taunt with an answer.

'Want to leave?' Franco drawled when she rejoined him.

Now, there's a leading question! Cut and run...or stay. 'Soon.' She offered him a brilliant smile. 'After I roll the dice.' And ensure Famke doesn't see me slink away like a wounded warrior.

Luck had apparently taken a holiday, for the dice didn't roll in her favour, and she stood back, choosing to watch rather than participate.

It was almost midnight when Franco eased the Mercedes onto the main road and headed towards suburban Toorak. The night was clear, with an indigo sky sprinkled with stars indicating the promise of a fine day.

The Cirque du Soleil had been fantastic, and she said so as he garaged the car, adding, 'It was kind of you to invite Tom and Shannay.'

'My pleasure.'

They ascended the stairs together, and entered the bedroom.

The stilettos were the first to go, followed by her tights. The jacket, the camisole...the make-up, then the pins from her hair.

He followed her action in discarding his clothes, watching idly as the sophisticated image gradually diminished as she loosened her hair and shook it free.

Petite, and possessed of a false air of fragility that was at odds with her inner strength. A pocket dynamo, Franco mused, who, given her private wealth, could easily have become a social butterfly intent on working the social scene. Instead, she'd chosen 'the firm', unhesitating in her determination to succeed. Driven, as he was, to preserve and foster their heritage.

Women he'd slept with in the past had delighted in wearing figure-hugging nightwear in silk and lace...or posed naked for his pleasure.

Yet this woman defied the norm and chose an oversized cotton tee-shirt, which, dammit, made her look infinitely more sexy than any silk or lace concoction ever could.

'Leave it.'

Gianna's fingers stilled from gathering her hair together prior to twisting it into a braid. 'It gets tangled if I leave it undone.'

Franco crossed to stand behind her and removed her hands, then gently thread his fingers through its silky length.

Liquid fire pooled deep within and slowly rippled through her body as it brought her *alive* in a way only he could achieve.

He used his fingers to work a subtle circular massage, probing, soothing, until she almost sighed from pleasure.

It felt so *good*, and a soft sound purred from her throat as he eased forward to her temples, then worked his way down to her neck, her shoulders.

He bunched her hair away from her nape, then pressed his lips to a sensitive curve, sought the hollow at the edge of her neck, then pulled the tee-shirt free and curved an arm beneath her breasts.

The desire to tease and torment him was uppermost as she turned in his arms and began a tantalising exploration that had the breath hissing through his teeth.

Feather-light touches along highly sensitised skin, and she glimpsed the clench of muscle, the ripple of sinew as she tested his control.

Primitive pleasure, intensely tactile, incredibly intimate.

Not content, she brushed her lips in a delicate pattern over his chest, seeking a male nipple and savouring it, nibbling a little, then catching the sensitive nub with the edge of her teeth.

A husky groan sounded deep in his throat as she transferred her attention to its twin and rendered a similar pleasure before trailing to his navel, exploring it with the tip of her tongue, then brushing a path over his taut stomach to the dark silky hair couching his fully aroused penis.

Size and strength, its rigidity fascinated her, and her inner muscles clenched in anticipation of Franco's possession. The long slow slide, the withdrawal, the deep thrust as he began a pagan rhythm that carried her with him to the edge, held her there, then tipped her over to join him in raw primal sensation so intense she cried out with it.

'Enough.' His voice was a barely audible groan as he hauled her high against him and possessed her mouth with his own.

In one easy move she wrapped her legs round his waist and held on, exulting in the power and the passion as he took her on an evocative ride, utilising all the primitive sexual energy of good sex.

Very good sex, she conceded much later as she lay spent in his arms.

Santo Giancarlo adored company, and he was a generous and gregarious host. Whereas Anamaria Castelli was a stickler for order and everything in its place, Santo seemed content to live with ordered clutter…ordered by virtue of his housekeeper's diligent efforts to maintain a semblance of tidiness.

His home, he assured everyone, was *his*, and all he required was comfort, cleanliness and good food. The grounds and gardens, however, were something else.

It was hardly surprising the grandparents clashed on every level, Gianna determined as she walked around the garden at Santo's side. The one exception was their love of gardening.

Yet the comparison between grandfather and grandson was evident.

Icons in the corporate industry, driven to succeed. To look at both men, it was easy to see the connection...the same tall frame, chiselled features, the direct gaze that saw much, and beneath the surface the hard ruthless edge that set them apart from their peers.

Thirty years from now would Franco assume his grandfather's persona, and take *life* in both hands and shake it a little?

Would she be around to know? Or would she have passed her use-by date and joined the first wives' club? Superceded by the latest young thing in eye candy?

'You're *thinking*.'

Gianna met Santo's musing gaze. 'That's a no-no?'

'Depends on the importance of the thought.'

Well, it was pretty difficult *not* to accord importance to the woman threatening to tear her heart apart!

Worse, she couldn't discuss any of her fears and insecurities about the survival of their marriage with Franco. What if he hesitated in providing reassurance or brushed off her concerns as unreasonable?

'You can bank on Franco's loyalty.'

Where had that cryptic statement come from? Was she so transparent?

'I know.' *Did she?* What a joke! She had serious doubts about her ability to know anything any more.

'We've exhausted the garden,' Santo said gently. 'And you haven't confided what's worrying you.'

Was it that obvious? She'd have to smile a lot, and try harder playing the 'pretend I'm absolutely fine' game. 'Why do you imagine anything is?'

'Put it down to a lot of practice reading between the lines of the female mind.'

It was on the tip of her tongue to ask what he thought he saw in hers...except the answer might not be what she wanted to hear.

Franco was on his cellphone when they entered the lounge, and he cut the call…the third in succession since his grandfather had led Gianna outdoors on a tour of the garden.

He took in the faint edginess apparent, the too-bright smile, and his eyes narrowed slightly. The likelihood Santo might have said something to upset her didn't exist. So what…?

'Tell me about the Cirque du Soleil,' Santo encouraged as they did justice to the excellent *pasta al forno* his housekeeper had prepared.

'It was incredible,' Gianna enthused, and described the high points…*sans* Famke's intervention.

They shared coffee in the lounge, and around nine Franco indicated the need to leave.

'I have a report to prepare.' One that would involve at least an hour of his time. And he was due to catch an early flight to Sydney in the morning, with meetings scheduled all day, followed by negotiations Tuesday, and hopefully a satisfactory resolution. Something he'd fight tooth and nail for…and walk away from if he had to.

Gianna brushed a kiss to Santo's cheek as Franco fired the ignition.

'Will you wrap everything up tomorrow?'

He spared her a glance as he cleared the avenue and swung on to the main road. 'No. Is that a problem?'

'Of course not.'

Did Famke know he was going to be out of town? Hot on the tail of that question came another… Was the actress planning on meeting him in Sydney?

The mere thought it could be a possibility nearly destroyed her.

Gianna didn't offer a further word during the short drive home, and she merely inclined her head as he reiterated his intention to complete the report.

She'd take a book to bed and read for a while in the hope she'd become immersed in the story, the fictional characters…to the extent Famke's image couldn't intrude.

Fat chance, when her head was already filled with the unwanted vision of Famke and Franco wrapped in each other's arms!

It was almost midnight when Franco entered the bedroom, and he undressed, then slid in beside her and gathered her close.

She didn't stir, and he resisted the temptation to tease her into wakefulness.

There was an advantage in being kept busy, Gianna determined as she handled one call after another, participated in a conference call and attended a meeting.

As the day progressed it was impossible not to spare a thought to how Franco intended to spend the evening. A business dinner…or dinner *à deux* in his hotel suite with Famke?

Oh, for heaven's sake! Talk about paranoia! There was every chance Famke knew nothing of Franco's business schedule.

Yet within a week the actress had managed to inveigle a spot as guest at a charity dinner, expose photographs in the social column of the city's newspaper, appear at Saturday evening's show…and let's not forget the few verbal warnings.

Famke's intention was crystal-clear.

Franco's reaction, however, was not.

Gianna's cellphone rang, and she picked up to discover Shannay on the line.

'Feel like taking in dinner and a movie tonight?'

'Tom—?'

'Said Franco's out of town, and you might feel like a girls' night out.'

Good friends were wonderful! 'You're on,' she agreed at once. 'Give me a time and place, and I'll meet you there.'

Shannay reeled off both with alacrity, and as soon as Gianna cut the call she immediately made another to Rosa.

The day suddenly took a brighter turn, and she took time to go home to shower and change before meeting Shannay at Southbank.

'A glass of wine with dinner. We both have to drive,' Shannay determined as they perused the menu, made a selection, then gave their order.

'OK…now, *give*,' Shannay demanded as soon as the waiter had moved away from their table.

Gianna raised both eyebrows. 'Be specific.'

'Famke.'

'Ah.'

'What are you doing about her?'

'Aside from wanting to tell her go jump?'

Shannay leaned back in her chair. 'Thank God. For a moment I had serious doubts.'

'She and Franco—'

'I know. But that was ages ago, and it was over before it even got started.'

She had a vivid memory of *weeks* rather than days. Anguish, heartache, *pain*. Imagination was a terrible thing!

'But now she's divorced and—'

'Has Franco in her sights.' Shannay took a sip of wine, and became contemplative. 'Not that she stands a chance.'

'You think?'

'Why?' Shannay argued. 'When he has *you*?'

'Shannay, I adore you. But let's not forget my marriage isn't exactly a love match.'

'Isn't it?'

'Maybe on my part, but not on his.'

'Oh…*fiddlesticks*.'

'You've arrived at this conclusion *because*?'

The waiter delivered their starter, and Shannay paused until he'd moved out of earshot.

'I've seen the way he looks at you.'

Gianna surveyed her friend over the rim of her glass. 'Lust.'

'There are those who are not blind, but cannot see.'

'Uh-huh. And there are those who only see what they want to see.'

Shannay lifted both hands, palms out. 'OK, let's break for a while.' Her features became serious. 'But if you think I'm done, forget it.'

The fact Shannay didn't bring up the subject again until after they'd finished the main course said much for her restraint.

'You can't allow Famke to see her strategy is getting to you.'

'I'm working on it.'

'Don't underestimate her,' Shannay warned. 'She's a bitch.'

'Already got that one.'

The waiter appeared, cleared their plates, and queried dessert preferences.

'Fresh fruit, and coffee—black.'

Shannay checked her watch. 'We should move soon if we want to make the movie on time.'

They made it into the cinema just as the lights began to dim. Light and funny, with good acting, believable characters and wonderful dialogue, the movie provided plenty of laughs.

'Coffee?' Shannay suggested as they emerged into the main foyer. 'You're in no hurry to get home, and Tom indicated pumpkin time.'

Gianna looked askance.

'Cinderella…midnight?'

She should have got it. The fact she hadn't said much for her state of mind!

Coffee—decaf otherwise she wouldn't sleep—sounded like a good idea, and she entered a trendy café at Shannay's side.

'Looks as though everyone has the same idea.'

It was crowded, and they managed to find a table more by luck than anything else, and ordered two decaf lattes.

'What you need to do,' Shannay began, 'is be friendly with the enemy. In public.'

'Don't give up, do you?'

'Hey, we shared kindergarten, boarding school, and we did the bridesmaid thing at each other's wedding. I'm first in line to kick butt.'

'Loyalty is a wonderful thing, and I thank you for it,' Gianna said with a tinge of amusement.

'But it's your butt to kick?'

'Yes.'

'Shannay. Gianna. Two of my favourite women.'

The faintly accented voice was familiar, and they turned in unison to see Gervaise Champeliere and his brother, Emile. Gervaise indicated the two empty chairs.

'There don't appear to be any empty tables. May we join you?'

'Of course.'

'No women in tow tonight?' Shannay teased after they'd placed an order for coffee.

'A business dinner.' Gervaise effected a light shrug. 'A walk in the night air seemed a good idea, and maybe a coffee...'

Two powerful businessmen, friends and associates of both Tom and Franco. What could be more pleasant than to share coffee and conversation for a while?

The only down moment was provided by a photographer, who reeled off several shots as they were about to leave. One of the social paparazzi on the night prowl, hoping for a scoop.

A telling caption would turn innocence into compromise, for the name of the game was to sell copy.

Gervaise murmured something vicious beneath his breath.

'Well, that was fun.'

Emile tossed a note onto the table to cover the bill. 'Where are you parked?'

They reached Gianna's BMW first, and the girls hugged, murmured mutual thanks, and within minutes Gianna entered the main stream of traffic.

It was almost midnight when she entered the house, and she checked the answering machine, discovered two messages, neither of which was from Franco. Her cellphone wasn't registering any SMS texts, and the doubts she'd held at bay over the past few hours rose to the surface, invading her mind and eventually her dreams.

CHAPTER EIGHT

WHAT price fame? Gianna wondered cynically as she opened the morning newspaper and flipped to the social page. For there, featured in a prominent position, was a photograph taken inside the café the night before.

Four people, happy, with an implied intimacy that didn't exist. The caption endorsed the image, employing subtle speculation that caused Gianna to close the newspaper in disgust. The social grapevine would have a field-day as gossip became embellished and blown out of all proportion.

She was all too familiar with the process.

Syndication posed the question whether the photograph might also appear in one of the Sydney newspapers. Next, if Franco might see it before she had the opportunity to explain.

Which meant she should make a phone call and alert him.

Her cellphone pealed and she checked the caller ID, recognised Shannay's number, and picked up.

'It's in.' Her voice was brisk. 'Tom suggests damage control. He'll run it by Franco. You OK?'

'About to walk out the door. I'll call you later.'

She had Franco's cellphone number on speed-dial, and she hit it, only to have the call go straight to the message bank.

Damn. He could be in the shower, having breakfast, or…indulging in a bedroom romp with Famke?

Don't go there, an inner voice screamed.

It took effort to bank down the image and mentally discard it.

Focus on what you have to do, she bade herself firmly. Right now, that involves going in to the office to work.

She almost made it...almost. Would have, if she hadn't opened an incoming text message as she sat in traffic waiting for a set of lights to change.

Loved photo. Sydney wonderful. Famke.

Gianna tossed the cellphone onto the passenger seat with an audible growl of anger. What had taken her so long?

Until Franco had left the hotel suite and taken a cab to wherever he was due for the day? After Famke had ensured he'd sighted the appropriate page in the morning newspaper?

Dammit, she had no problem visualising *that* scenario in vivid detail.

To say it ruined her day was an understatement. She didn't know whether to weep, rage...or throw the worst hissy fit in known history!

Instead, she buried herself in work, made the necessary calls...except to Franco. *Him* she'd deal with in person!

Anamaria phoned, with an invitation to morning tea on Saturday.

Lunch was a salad sandwich eaten at her desk, and she was so *businesslike* during a mid-afternoon marketing meeting it was almost a joke. Except the façade was the only thing that permitted her to hold everything together.

The cracks began to appear as she battled peak-hour traffic, and she hammered her car horn twice, muttered something ugly beneath her breath…when normally she would have contained herself.

Franco's Mercedes wasn't in the garage, and she didn't know whether to be disappointed or pleased at gaining extra time ahead of initiating a confrontation.

Yet he could drive up any time soon, and with this in mind she went through to the kitchen. It was better Rosa wasn't within earshot when she launched into combat mode!

Food was the last thing on her mind, but she gave Rosa the necessary assurances regarding dinner before going upstairs to change into sweats and a pair of trainers, then she caught her hair back in a ponytail and descended the stairs to the gym.

A workout might serve to channel some of her anger, and she did time on the treadmill, utilised hand-weights, used the rowing machine, the Exercycle, then she donned boxing gloves and worked up a sweat pounding the punching bag.

Gianna was almost done when Franco entered the gym, and she didn't break until he moved into her line of vision.

Seconds were all it took to register he'd abandoned the trappings of formal business apparel for sweats and trainers.

'You have reason to go so hard with this?'

'It's a substitute for *you.*'

He reached out and stilled her flailing arms with galling ease. 'How so?'

She glared at him. 'As if you don't know!'

Franco caught the pent-up anger, the darkness evident in her eyes, and tightened his grasp. 'Gervaise has been in touch and filled me in with—'

'This isn't about Gervaise.'

His features hardened. 'Then what the hell is it about?'

'Let go of my hands.'

He did...only to visibly wince when she lashed out with an unexpected punch, and he fielded another before it could connect.

'You want to fight with me?'

Gianna ignored the silky threat evident. '*Yes*, damn you!'

The top of her head barely reached his shoulder, and he had to be twice her weight. 'Pick something at which you might have half a chance.'

Kick-boxing wouldn't cut it. He had the expertise, longer and more powerful legs, and he'd never give her an opening to get in close enough to connect.

Her growl of frustration was very real, and her eyes gleamed with anger as he pulled off her gloves.

If looks could kill, he'd be dead already.

'You're trying my patience.'

She'd tortured herself with painful images all day. A strenuous workout had done nothing to diminish the anguish, and she desperately wanted him to *pay*.

'So...bite me.'

'Now, there's a provocative thought.'

Gianna slapped his face. Hard. And nearly died at the cold anger evident.

'You have two minutes to explain yourself.'

Two angry people facing off. How much worse could it get?

'One minute fifty seconds.'

Belligerent temper wasn't her thing. Never had been. So why resort to it now?

Because she couldn't bear the thought of losing him...yet was terribly afraid she might.

'Gianna.' His voice held a silky warning that prompted her into speech.

'Famke sent me an SMS informing me that she spent the night with you in Sydney.'

Dear heaven. Did he have any idea how *tortured* she felt by it?

'You believed her?'

She'd tried so hard not to! Even given the actress's propensity for diabolical behaviour, the SMS had provided that one grain of doubt. By the end of the day, that was all it had taken to set her mind into overdrive.

'She's an ex-lover, she wants you, and she's made it clear she's prepared to do anything to get you.' Without a care if she destroys me emotionally in the process.

'Therefore making it a *fait accompli*?' His eyes were dark, and tinged with latent anger. 'Aren't you forgetting something?'

Gianna looked at him in silence.

'Famke might have a picture in mind...but I don't choose to be in it.'

'You might care to tell her that!'

'I already have.'

Could she believe him? *Should* she?

'Whatever happened to trust?'

If I was secure in your love, trust wouldn't be an issue. Words she couldn't bring herself to utter without revealing the depth of her feelings. And she didn't want to give him that power.

'You think I'd break my vow of fidelity?'

I don't know.

'If Famke flew in to Sydney, I was unaware of it.' His voice reminded her of silk-sheathed steel. 'You have my word. It should be enough.'

He crossed to the rowing machine, and she refused to observe, even for a few seconds, his impressive muscles flex as he began to work the machine.

Instead, she went upstairs, stripped off her sweats and took a leisurely shower, then she donned casual jeans, added a top, and sequestered herself in her study.

The thought of food made her feel almost physically ill, and she opened her laptop and set to work.

Shannay phoned around eight-thirty, and began without preamble, 'You were supposed to return my call.'

How could she have forgotten? 'I'm sorry. It's been quite a day.' A gross understatement if ever there was one.

'Tom has made a reservation for the four of us to dine together tomorrow night. Franco has the details.'

She tried for enthusiasm, and made it…just. 'Great.'

'Did you receive any flak re the newspaper photo?'

'A call from my grandmother, suggesting morning tea Saturday. I'm expecting words of wisdom together with a reminder to observe circumspection at all times.' She paused. 'You?'

'Mother, ditto. No breath of scandal… etc.'

Shannay ended the call, and Gianna put in a further two hours' work, then shut down the laptop and retired for the night.

Alone. Of Franco there was no sign, and she slid into bed and snapped off the lamp.

There was a note written in Franco's script propped on the table when Gianna went down to breakfast next morning.

Meeting Tom and Shannay, six-thirty, city

Damage control. Two couples, projecting happiness and togetherness, ensuring they gained the necessary exposure to warrant a photograph in the social page of tomorrow's newspaper. Thus contradicting media innuendo regarding the state of each marriage.

It sounded like a plan.

Had Franco alerted Rosa they would be dining out?

Gianna wrote a note and attached it with a magnet to the kitchen fridge.

The restaurant numbered high as one of the city's finest, and was deliberately chosen because it was a known haunt of the rich and famous.

'You think this is going to work?'

Shannay lifted her crystal flute and tipped it in silent salute. 'Who cares?' She offered an elfin smile. 'We get to enjoy each other's company, eat fine food and drink champagne.'

Gianna touched the rim of her flute to Shannay's in agreement. 'What more could anyone ask?'

Her friend's mouth assumed a mischievous tilt. 'Gervaise, Emile, and call it a party?'

'That might be taking things a bit far.'

'You think?'

'Behave,' Tom admonished.

'It's been a difficult day,' Shannay confided. 'My stepdaughter demoted me to the stepmother-from-hell because I failed to agree purple is the hair colour of choice with the *in* crowd. This was at breakfast, which is not my best time of the day. A brief respite during school hours, after which my stepson decided to test me by assuring an ear-stud *is* a permissible accessory to his school uniform.'

Gianna endeavoured to hide a smile. 'Oh, dear.'

'Yesterday,' Shannay continued, making the most of her moment, 'one of his friends said I was cute, and earned himself a bloodied nose. This, of course, did not go down well and gained a detention.'

'Totally your fault you were under the right table when *cute* was being handed out.'

Shannay fixed her with a telling look. '*You* are supposed to be my very best friend. Shall I go on?'

'Must you?' Gianna teased.

'There's more. The ultimate sin for a stepmother is to wear a size smaller than her stepdaughter.'

'Tears and tantrums duly evolved,' Tom elaborated. 'And yet she wants babies.'

'Ours will be different.'

'Darling, they too will grow to be teen-agers.'

'What a sobering thought.'

Tom engaged Franco in stock market graphs, and Gianna considered the dessert menu, then opted for tea.

As the waiter moved away she caught sight of a camera flash, and she alerted quietly, 'Paparazzi.'

The photographer was quick...he probably had to be in order to cover several hot spots in an evening.

'Mission accomplished,' Shannay declared as he disappeared out through the door.

They lingered a while, enjoying the camaraderie of established friendship.

'We must do this again.' Franco caught hold of Gianna's hand and threaded his fingers through her own as Shannay bestowed a hug.

'Lunch, some time soon?'

'Call me.'

They strolled in different directions to where their cars were parked. The city streets would soon come alive as diners emerged from various restaurants. But for now it was relatively quiet, and Gianna leaned back against the headrest and closed her eyes.

She had a busy few days ahead of her. So too did Franco. He worked long hours, rising early to do a daily workout in the gym, and he travelled frequently. Interstate, overseas. Wheeling and dealing, maintaining that essential edge to keep Giancarlo-Castelli ahead of the rest.

*   *   *

Summoned to report, Gianna mused as she slid her BMW to a halt beneath the portico attached to Anamaria's imposing home with little doubt as to the reason behind the invitation to share morning tea.

Ten minutes, possibly fifteen, she calculated, before her grandmother launched into chastising mode.

Less…which meant this must be more serious than she'd first thought. Worse, a folded newspaper lay within hand's reach.

'Gianna,' Anamaria began without preamble as she indicated the pertinent photograph, 'what were you *thinking*?'

Her explanation wasn't going to fly… sometimes the most simple truth never did. However, she could only try.

'I met Shannay for dinner and a movie. We went for coffee later. Two friends were among fellow customers, and they joined us.'

'Two *male* friends.' Anamaria barely gave pause. 'With whom you were photographed.'

Why did she feel like a recalcitrant pupil being called to account by a headmistress? 'It was spontaneous, and completely innocent.'

'Of course.'

Well, thank heavens for small mercies! And a degree of familial loyalty!

'However, that isn't how it appears. The caption gives cause for speculation.' Her grandmother drew in an imperious breath and slowly released it. 'And merely adds fuel to that foolish actress's *contretemps* with the media.'

A discreet knock at the door heralded the housekeeper's arrival with a loaded tea tray, from which Anamaria indicated she herself would serve...and immediately did so.

'It would be advantageous if an announcement could be made.'

The morning just got worse.

'Prior to conception?' It was impossible to keep the edge of cynicism from her voice, and her grandmother's eyes narrowed.

'The inability to conceive bothers you?'

There was never going to be a better time. 'It bothers me that you continually stress the issue.'

Anamaria appeared to straighten her shoulders and draw in breath...with no visible sign of movement. An optical illusion?

'You do...sleep together?'

'You mean...have sex?' It was difficult not to burst into laughter, except it might veer towards the hysterical. 'With active frequency.' Oh, why not go the full distance? 'And, no, we don't use protection.'

Was that a tinge of colour beneath the delicate rouge on her grandmother's cheeks?

'Can we agree for you to leave the subject alone?' Gianna said gently. 'It's become tiresome.'

'Very well. I apologise.'

She couldn't recall a time when Anamaria had offered an apology to anyone. Certainly not within her presence. 'Thank you.'

CHAPTER NINE

IT WAS almost midday when Gianna left, and she visited a few exclusive boutiques along Toorak Road, then took time to eat something healthy for lunch before heading for an antiques auction.

One of several such auctions held throughout the year, today's event featured select hand-crafted pieces and formed part of a collection.

A number of cars lined the suburban avenue, and she joined many potential bidders intent on viewing the various items on display in the old, beautifully kept home.

A deceased estate, with family choosing to sell.

Gianna was almost moved to tears at the thought of several exquisite rosewood pieces being separated and taken to different houses, when they so obviously belonged together.

Fool. They're inanimate pieces of wood, they have no soul... But the craftsmanship was superb, carved with loving hands and an empathy with the tool.

Then she saw it...a small desk, with a delicate inlayed top and beautifully carved legs. Perfection.

Gianna traced gentle fingers along its surface, felt the smoothness of the wood, and fell in love with it.

'Pretty, isn't it?'

I don't believe it. Famke? *Here?*

Without doubt, the actress's appearance at every turn went way past the possibility of coincidence.

'Why don't I give you a copy of our social calendar?' she ventured silkily. 'Then you won't have to knock yourself out discovering my every move?'

Famke gave her a withering look. 'Darling, who cares about *you*?'

'Of course. I'm merely the appendage inconveniently attached to Franco.'

'Yes.'

Succinct, and delivered with a poisonous sting. So what else was new?

It was way past time she did a little stinging of her own! 'How is your daughter?'

Blue eyes assumed the iciness of an arctic floe. 'My daughter has nothing to do with this.'

Gianna arched an eyebrow. 'No?' Her pause was deliberate. 'I assume you've left her in very good care while you're absent on the other side of the world?'

'She has a nanny.'

'Poor child. Deprived of a mother who pursues what she wants…professionally and personally.'

'I share custody with her father.'

Gianna pretended to examine her nails. 'Aren't you afraid you might have your custody reduced, or even lose it completely?'

'Are you *threatening* me?'

'Not at all. Just making conversation.'

'I'm entitled to a life of my own.'

'Yes, you are. But not with my husband.'

'But then, he's never really been *yours*…has he?'

She was never going to have the last word. So she made it easy, and simply turned and walked away.

Not so easy to dispel her irritation. So far the day was turning out just peachy…

The auction began promptly at two-thirty, with spirited bidding and high closing figures as one by one the items were sold.

The beautiful desk Gianna coveted attracted several bids, soon diminishing to four, then three, and finally two serious bidders…

It became a game, and all about winning, as she topped every bid Famke made, going ridiculously high in a room strangely quiet apart from the auctioneer's voice.

Those present caught there was something more going on, and soon there were whispers, conjecture Gianna chose to block out.

A male voice joined the bidding, a voice she recognised only too well, and she spared Franco a quick glance, then looked away.

That *he* might want the desk for himself was ludicrous. So why was he bidding? The more pertinent question had to be for *whom* the desk was intended?

Gianna registered the excessively high bid and made her final call. It had gone way past sensible bidding and become a pathetic game between two women determined to outdo each other.

Well, she was done. Over it.

Franco made an astronomical bid that drew a collective gasp from those gathered in the room… followed by an ensuing silence signifying his success, and the bidding was closed.

'Franco!'

Famke's exuberance was overwhelming, including as it did the wrapping of her arms round his shoulders. However, the overt kissy thing to each cheek went way over the top.

Although, to do him justice, he immediately extricated himself and caught hold of Gianna's hand in a bone-crushing grip.

The temptation to wrench free was difficult to resist, and she dug her nails in *hard* as a silent protest. An action which resulted in Franco threading his fingers through her own.

Famke, who should have registered their public solidarity and melted into the crowd, merely tucked her hand beneath his arm and hung on.

Flanked by two woman...one of whom was his wife, the other his former lover. It resulted in a photographic moment which irked Gianna no end.

Orchestrated by Famke?

Or was she becoming delusional? Surely that was Famke's field?

When in doubt…*smile*. She could do that. Anything less would send the gossip grapevine into overdrive.

Even Franco's deliberate action in removing Famke's hand did little to ease the anger simmering beneath the surface.

She wanted to leave and escape the veiled conjecture, except she was too well-schooled in the need for public unity. In private, however, she intended to nail him to the wall!

If he thought brushing a soothing thumbpad across the veins at her wrist would diminish her frayed temper, he was sorely mistaken.

The auction continued, with Franco successfully bidding for an exquisite leg sofa table.

Famke, not to be outdone, took an active part in the bidding, choosing to defer to Franco on occasion via an expressive lift of an eyebrow, a smile in a deliberate attempt to claim his attention.

It hardly mattered he didn't respond. The implication was there, and that was enough.

'I'll go organise the relevant details,' Franco indicated when the auction came to an end, and Gianna proffered a sweet smile.

'I'll go on ahead.'

'This won't take long. Wait for me.'

Life a dutiful wife? Stay here and watch Famke take every opportunity to play-act the coquette? Not if she could help it!

She kept the smile in place, and waited only until he was engaged in paperwork before slipping quietly out through the door.

The BMW purred to life, and she headed towards the city and Southbank, where she could wander the boardwalk, choose a café along the river-front and sip a latte. Anything to delay going home for a while.

The insistent peal of her cellphone provided a momentary distraction she chose to ignore as she slid into a parking space and cut the engine.

Franco, she determined as she checked Caller ID.

She should probably send him a courtesy text message…no, dammit, he could suffer a little!

Another call came through as she sat sipping coffee at an outdoor umbrella-covered table overlooking the river, and she let the call go to the message bank.

Ten minutes later her cellphone beeped with an incoming text message.

State your location. F

Really! As if she would meekly comply any time soon!

Gianna studied the cityscape, then idly observed the traffic flow before turning her attention to the people strolling the boardwalk.

Young couples, groups… It was Saturday evening—what better than to wander a little, eat a meal, then take in a movie, a play, or go bar-hopping before transferring to a party?

A waiter hovered, checking if she was ready to order food, and she studied the menu, chose something light and requested bottled water.

Famke's image remained a tangible entity as Gianna did a mental rerun of the afternoon.

Surely Franco saw through the actress's guile?

In the business arena he'd earned a reputation as a merciless strategist. But when it came to a conniving woman? Especially one he'd bedded in the past?

The waiter delivered the bottled water, uncapped and poured the chilled liquid. Her hand shook a little as she reached for the glass, and she swore beneath her breath.

Gianna became conscious of the sounds around her, the background music and snatches of conversation as people passed by. The excited shriek of a child, the distant traffic, an occasional horn-blast.

The early-evening air turned cool as a brisk breeze rolled over the riverfront. Waiters began lighting numerous heated standard lamps, and within minutes she was served with her meal.

Artistically presented, it looked delectable, and she savoured the aroma before forking a portion to taste.

After a few mouthfuls she pushed the plate to one side. An action which soon caught the waiter's attention.

'There is something wrong with your meal?'

'It's fine,' she assured him. 'I'm not very hungry.'

'Would you like me to remove the plate? Perhaps you would like coffee?'

Maybe a different hot drink? 'Tea?' She quickly added her preference.

Her cellphone pealed with an incoming

call, and it went straight to the message bank. Minutes later it signified a text message. Franco.

Please respond.

It was the *please* that did it, and within seconds she keyed back.

Home later. G.

Within seconds back came:

Want company?

No.

She wasn't ready to face him yet.

There was no point wandering aimlessly, and on the spur of the moment she opted to take in a movie. Preferably something light and funny.

Walking alone in the city after dark wasn't a good idea, and she retraced her steps to her car, then drove to a cinemaplex, chose a movie, and tried to lose herself in the plot, the characters, the comedy.

Without much success. And it was almost eleven when she reached Toorak and garaged the car.

The slim hope Franco might have gone to bed and, please Lord, be asleep, was ill-founded, for when she entered the foyer he was there waiting for her, his hands thrust into trouser pockets.

Looking, Gianna determined, a little less than his usual well-groomed self. Unless she was mistaken he hadn't changed clothes, though his tie was gone, his shirt buttons were loosened, the cuffs rolled back, and his hair looked ruffled.

Concern? For *her*? Or was it merely contained anger he would unleash any minute soon?

'Perhaps you'd care to offer an explanation?'

His drawled query sounded like silk being razed by steel, and she unconsciously stiffened beneath the dark intensity of his gaze.

There was nothing like facing the issue head-on. 'I had a meal at Southbank, then went to the movies.' Her eyes speared his. 'I needed some time alone.'

'You could have answered your cell-phone.'

'I did. Eventually.' She stepped past him and headed towards the stairs. 'Goodnight.'

'Don't ever do that again.'

Gianna turned and shot him an indignant glare. 'Or...*what*?'

'Don't push it.' His silky warning slithered the length of her spine.

'Same goes.'

The silence was almost audible as she challenged him with fearless disregard.

She was a piece of work, a conflicting mix of strength and fragility, and she tore at his emotions in a way no woman had been able to achieve.

Her eyes raked his tall frame, settled briefly on the sensuous curve of his mouth and killed the thought of how it felt on her own. She tilted her head in a defiant gesture.

'Right now I don't feel inclined to do verbal battle.'

His ensuing silence had more effect than anything he could have said.

For a moment she felt the surge of victory, only for it to deflate as she undressed and made ready for bed.

A warm shower did nothing to ease the tension, and she emerged into the bedroom unsure whether to feel relieved or peeved Franco was nowhere in sight.

She slid between the sheets, switched off the bedside lamp and lay staring at the darkened ceiling until sleep finally claimed her.

CHAPTER TEN

MONDAY became one of those days when whatever could go wrong, did. The planet Mercury in retrograde? The Irish gremlin, Murphy, causing mischief and mayhem?

Maybe both, Gianna decided grimly as her hairdrier refused to heat, she laddered one pair of tights and put a fingernail through a second pair. Breakfast didn't happen, and she filched a banana and tub of yoghurt from the fridge to eat at her desk, then fought bumper-to-bumper traffic into the city.

Appointments, fine-tuned to dovetail during the morning, consequently backed up and overlapped, causing her PA to issue one apology after another, which Gianna reiterated in person.

Lunch was something her PA sent out for and Gianna nibbled at between client appointments and phone calls. But mid-afternoon she'd caught up, and she began inputting data into the laptop. God willing, she'd be done around five.

Franco's text-message— *Business meeting. Don't wait dinner*—just she walked out through the door barely raised an eyebrow, although a call on her cellphone as she sat stationary at a set of traffic lights on Toorak Road did.

'Don't wait up, darling,' a familiar feminine voice informed her with a light laugh. 'I plan to keep him out very late.'

Famke.

It didn't take much to do the maths…but was the answer the right one, or merely another attempt by the actress to cause trouble?

Gianna's first instinct was to ring Franco and demand the truth, except the opportunity was lost as the traffic began to move, forcing her to wait until she reached home.

When she did make the call, it went straight to his message bank, and for a second she hesitated...leave a message, or just cut the connection?

Cut, she decided, and endeavoured to ignore the pain in the region of her heart.

The possibility Franco might be dining with Famke almost destroyed her. To imagine them sharing wine, food...and intimate looks across the table, the anticipation, the promise. It almost tore her apart.

However, there were practicalities to deal with, and she entered the kitchen, greeted Rosa and relayed Franco was joining a colleague for dinner.

It was truth by omission. 'Please, take the food and share it with Enrico.'

'But what about you?' the housekeeper responded with concern. 'You need to eat.'

The mere thought of food made her feel ill. 'I had a substantial lunch.' Another untruth, but she didn't want to offer an explanation. 'I'll fix something light later on.' A smile came easily. 'Go.'

Rosa looked doubtful. 'Are you sure?'

'Positive.'

What she needed, she decided after Rosa left, was something constructive to *do*. Shower first, she decided, then she'd change into jeans and tee-shirt, maybe turn on the television and channel-hop for a while.

It didn't work, for she still felt as restless as a caged animal, beset with a tension that ate at her nerves as she clock-watched and endeavoured not to let her imagination run riot.

She wanted to call someone...but *who*? Shannay? Except Shannay was attending a medical dinner with Tom.

Damn. She was dying here.

OK, so she'd retreat to her studio and paint.

Tucked between the garages and the house, the room was large, airy, and held everything she needed to indulge her artistic bent. It was a hobby, something that stirred her soul and lent an ability to express her emotions with paint on canvas.

It didn't take long to change into old jeans and top, and slip her feet into worn trainers, then she caught up her cellphone, some bottled water, and entered the studio.

There were a stack of CDs—mood music to help create the ambience she wanted. Soft, dreamy wind music, opera sung by Pavarotti, Bocelli…and, at the opposite end of the spectrum, hard rock.

Tonight she needed something with spirit, and preferably loud. Tempestuous.

Gianna set up a fresh canvas, selected paints…and began. Red, black, splashes of orange slowly took on an abstract form.

Expressive, explosive, it screamed some-thing a psychologist would undoubtedly have a field-day with in analytical interpre-tation.

Quite frankly, she didn't give a fig. The method of applying paint to canvas served as a mild catharsis, and she lost track of time.

It was there Franco found her, and she was unaware of his presence as he stood watching her body language, the sure brushstrokes. He caught her intense concentration, and the edge of temper transferred onto the canvas in something vivid and in stark contrast to anything she'd previously painted.

Music swelled to a crescendo, the tenor's voice unwavering as he reached and held the high note.

Fitting, Franco determined as he crossed to the CD player and lowered the sound.

It was then she paused, holding the brush away from the canvas as she turned to look at him.

He'd removed his jacket and held it hooked over one shoulder. He'd also loosened his tie and undone the top few buttons of his shirt.

Or had Famke loosened them for him?

Although he didn't, she had to admit, look like a man who'd very recently been well satisfied by a woman.

A faint laugh rose and died in her throat. Could you really *tell*?

'That looks interesting.'

She ignored his silky drawl for a few seconds, then offered, 'You think?'

He crossed to stand next to the canvas. 'I imagine there has to be a reason why you're closeted down here at eleven o'clock at night?'

Gianna shot him a wide-eyed look. 'You mean, instead of waiting in bed eagerly anticipating your return?'

His eyes narrowed. 'The meeting ran late.'

'Uh-huh.'

'You have a problem with that?'

'This…*meeting*,' she began with masked cynicism, 'took place in a restaurant?'

'You want me to go into detail with the menu?'

She closed her eyes, then opened them again. 'I'm sure Famke will delight in filling me in.'

'Famke told you she was with me?'

His query held a deadly softness she chose to ignore.

'Affirmative.' The glare she threw in his direction would have withered a lesser man.

Franco turned slightly and tossed his jacket over a nearby chair. 'Again you chose to take her word over mine?'

There was steel beneath the silky voice, and she drew herself up to her full height…which nowhere matched his. A fact which didn't deter her in the slightest.

'Dammit, her call came through a short time after your text message.'

'So you put two and two together, and came up with ten?'

'I tried to call you.'

'I had the phone on message bank, as it usually is during delicate negotiations.'

Delicate proved the catalyst, and she threw her brush at him, then followed it with a small pot of bright blue paint.

It hit his chest, cascaded paint over his shirt, then clattered down onto the tiled floor to roll in a drunken semi-circle before tilting to a stop.

He swore briefly, with emphasis, then he undid the remaining buttons, shrugged out of the shirt, bunched it up and binned it.

Without a further word he caught her up over one shoulder and strode from the studio.

'Put me down!' Gianna beat her hands against his back, with little effect. 'What do you think you're doing?'

'Taking you to bed.'

'The hell you are!'

'It's the one place where we're perfectly in accord.'

He entered the foyer, then made for the stairs, carrying her with an ease that was galling.

'Damn you!' She tried kicking him without success. 'If you don't put me down *now*, I'll—'

'What? Hit me again?'

'Worse.' A few possibilities flashed through her mind, and she fixed on at least one of them.

They reached the bedroom, and he crossed to the *en suite* bathroom, caught both her hands together, then stripped off his clothes and reached for the hem of her tee-shirt.

'Don't you dare!'

One tug, and the tee-shirt came off and hit the floor. She hadn't bothered with a bra, and she threw him a fulminating glare as he reached for the snap on her jeans.

'This is pathetic machoism!' Anger had crossed the line into fury, and her eyes blazed with it.

'Is that a new word?'

He skimmed her briefs free, and she bent her head and bit him, uncaring *where*, as long as she connected.

A vicious oath hissed between his teeth as he hauled her close and fastened his mouth over hers in angry possession.

One hand cupped her nape to hold fast her head, while the other slid to the base of her spine.

He gave no quarter as he plundered deep, wreaking a flagrant devastation of her senses until she beat her hands against his shoulders in an attempt to get him to desist.

Dear heaven. Nothing, *ever*, had come close to this.

She could hardly breathe, couldn't think, and a heartfelt groan rose in her throat, only to subside into a helpless whimper.

It seemed an age before he lifted his head, and he momentarily closed his eyes against the sight of her ravaged mouth.

'*Madre di Dio,*' he breathed in husky self-admonition.

His eyes were dark, almost black, and she swallowed nervously as he slid his hands to cup her face.

Her jaw hurt from the force of his invasion, and she stood perfectly still, mesmerised by the stark remorse evident in his expression.

You wanted to challenge him, a tiny voice intruded. Slip beneath the surface of his control and test his emotions. Unleash the tiger…

Well, now you have.

Gianna drew a deep shuddering breath, then released it. 'Please. Just…let me go.'

He brushed a gentle thumb over each cheek. 'Not in this lifetime.'

There wasn't an adequate word she could think to utter, and her lips trembled as he pressed his lips to her forehead, lingered there, then slipped down to cover her mouth with such incredible gentleness she wanted to weep.

Franco lifted his head a little and his eyes were dark, almost still as they met her own. 'If you want to check, ring the *à la carte* restaurant at the Langham Hotel and ask for the *maître d'*. He'll confirm I arrived with a male business associate at six-thirty and left three and a half hours later.'

Famke...spinning lies and creating bedlam?

Gianna became conscious of her nakedness, *his*, and she pushed free of him, then gathered up her clothes, shrugged into a robe, and walked to the door. 'I'm going to sleep in another room.'

'No.'

'You can't stop me.'

He could easily.

'But you won't,' she said quietly, reading his mind, and resisted the temptation to slam the door behind her.

It was doubtful any of the beds were made up, so she collected linen, a blanket, and crossed to the opposite wing in the house.

What price *principle*? she chastised beneath her breath as she plumped the pillow for the umpteenth time.

Sleep had never seemed more distant, yet she must have slipped into that somnolent state, for when she woke it was morning, and she was alone in the large bed she shared with Franco.

How on earth…?

Hot on the heels of wondering how she'd got there came the question as to whether they'd had sex.

She'd know. And she didn't feel…

Last night, painting, the scene in the studio, the bedroom…it all came back in vivid recall. So, too, did a degree of disquiet.

Had Franco told the truth?

Dammit, she needed to *know*.

Oh, Lord, she groaned minutes later. The time... what was the *time*? Another groan left her throat as she checked, and she hit the floor running, showered and dressed, then grabbed some fruit from the kitchen and made for the garage.

Most of the morning was spent making and taking calls, and she enjoyed a leisurely lunch at a nearby café before returning to the office to check out targets for a forthcoming marketing campaign.

Instant visual, Gianna determined, as she considered advertising mock-ups. Simple, striking, with words that got the message across.

Hmm, now, if they took the background from one, the words from another...maybe they'd have something.

She went to work, scanning images into her laptop, adjusting, merging, until she had it almost right.

Her cellphone pealed, and she picked it up automatically, without bothering to check Caller ID.

'It's Famke, darling.'

Wouldn't you just know it!

Civility was out. A stark, 'Yes?' sufficed in acknowledgment.

'Franco appears to be incommunicado.'

She didn't comment, and after a moment's silence the actress continued, 'Convey my gratitude for the desk. It's utterly gorgeous.'

Famke cut the call, and Gianna barely resisted the temptation to hurl the cellphone against the nearest wall.

Instead, she checked the number for the Langham Hotel, and eventually connected with the right person, who confirmed without hesitation Franco Giancarlo had indeed dined there the previous evening, in the company of a male colleague, and, yes, on checking the date and time imprint on the restaurant's copy receipt, the account had been paid at ten twenty-five pm.

Famke's lies were beginning to stack up.

Could the supposed gift of the desk be another?

It was almost six when Gianna slid her BMW to a halt in the garage. Franco's Mercedes wasn't there, which meant he was taking the late flight from Brisbane.

She went through to the kitchen, breathed in the delicious aroma of roast chicken, and felt the pangs of hunger. 'Hi, Rosa. Franco is going to be late.' She checked the time. 'Half an hour, OK? I'll go shower and change.'

The housekeeper offered a cheerful smile. 'There was a delivery for you. I had it put in your study.'

'Thanks.' A delivery? From whom? And why her study?

Tension coiled in her stomach as she ascended the stairs. Not another one of Famke's nasty surprises?

Gianna reached her study and opened the door, unsure quite what she'd find.

Ohmigod... She opened her mouth, then soundlessly closed it again.

There, perfectly positioned, was the antique desk on which Franco had bid a small fortune.

She didn't know whether to smile or cry...or both. For a moment she simply stood and drank it in, then she crossed the room and ran light fingers over the wood, lingered over the inlay, checked the beautifully fitted small drawers, the keys with their tassels.

A gift purchased by a man who knew how much it meant to her to own it. Not for its monetary value, but for its exquisite craftsmanship.

Pleasure unfurled deep inside and encompassed her body, crept into her heart and touched her soul.

Maybe she could begin to believe Famke was out of the picture. Was it possible the actress had never been *in* the picture?

Delusion, or deliberate meddling? An attempt to destroy…simply because Famke thought she could? For kicks? Revenge for Franco ending their relationship several years ago?

Gianna crossed to the phone and keyed in Franco's cellphone number, heard the muted burr, then he picked up.

'Gianna?'

The sound of his voice sent heat surging through her veins, and she was willing to swear her pulse accelerated to a faster beat. 'Thank you.'

'For what, specifically?'

'The desk.'

'It has arrived?'

There was no time like the present, and her fingers tightened on the phone. 'I owe you an apology.' Did he have any idea how much it cost her to say that?

'You called the Langham Hotel.'

She didn't pretend to misunderstand. 'Yes.'

'I'm about to board my flight.'

'OK.'

She heard his faint chuckle. 'Wait up for me, *cara*.'

He cut the connection before she had a chance to respond.

Her world suddenly became a brighter place, and she found herself humming beneath the shower. Attired in jeans and a cropped top, she returned downstairs, collected the delectable meal Rosa had prepared and took it out onto the terrace.

The sky was pale, almost opalescent in the pre-dusk light. Soon the sun would sink below the horizon and the colours gradually fade to a muted shade, then assume various shades of grey as the shadows fell.

Street lamps would provide pinpricks of light, and the tall city buildings would glow with varied coloured neon.

At this hour there was a stillness in the air, almost as if the remains of the day drew an imperceptible sigh before handing over to the darkness of night.

For it was then a different scene emerged, Gianna perceived. Some of it bright and vivacious as people dined, partied and entertained. While in the deep underbelly of the city there were those who arose with ill intent in mind, inhabiting areas where no sensible person would dare intrude.

It was pleasant to simply sit and absorb the evening tranquillity, Gianna mused. Right now Franco would be in mid-air, on a flight path to Melbourne. Two hours from now he'd be home.

There was a sense of anticipation, a spiral of sensation that began in her belly and gradually encompassed her entire body.

Could there be a chance he cared for her? *Really* cared?

She felt as if she was standing at the edge of a precipice…yet hesitant to take the final step in case she'd got it horribly wrong and Franco wasn't there to catch her.

Conflicting emotions didn't come close!

The light began to dim a little, and Gianna retreated indoors, secured the lock, carried her plate through to the kitchen, then went upstairs

She had yet to download e-mails, and she could work on the marketing strategy.

Franco found her there, deeply engrossed with data on the laptop screen, and he wandered into the room, crossed to her side and ran a light hand over her shoulder.

'Hi.' He leaned down and brushed his lips to her temple. 'Busy?'

She glanced up, met those dark eyes, and couldn't look away. 'Just…waiting for you.'

His smile melted her bones. 'Hold that thought while I go shower, hmm?'

He touched a light finger to the tip of her nose, then he turned and left the room before she should think of anything sensible to say.

The cursor blinked on the screen, and she made a few keystrokes, then closed the system down.

It was then she caught sight of the antique desk, and she closed her eyes in remorse at not having thanked him in person when it had been the first thing she'd intended to say.

Gianna entered the bedroom just as he emerged from the bathroom, a towel hitched low on his hips, his hair glistening damp from his shower.

Primitive male and intensely sexual, she accorded as he lifted his head and looked at her.

For a second the air seemed trapped in her lungs, and she couldn't move.

Ridiculous, she silently derided. She'd slept with him, shared every intimacy. Why so hesitant and shy now?

Did he sense it? See it?

Heavens, she fervently hoped not.

'The desk is beautiful. Thank you.'

'Come here.'

His voice held a gentleness that destroyed the fragile tenure of her control, and she couldn't move.

For a moment he simply looked at her, then he closed the distance between them and lifted a hand to trace the outline of her mouth…lips which trembled slightly beneath his touch.

'Famke has a lot to answer for.'

Ain't that the truth!

'She called you today.' It was a statement, not a query. 'Let me guess…she implied I bought the desk as a gift to her?'

'Yes.'

Franco's eyes hardened. 'She's a dangerous woman.'

Tell me something I don't know!

He cupped her face between his hands. 'I swear on my mother's grave…there's nothing between us except in Famke's mind.'

There was too much evidence against the actress, too many proven discrepancies for Gianna not to believe him.

'If she calls you again, refer her to me.'

Somehow she thought it a matter of *when*, not if, as she doubted the actress was anywhere near done.

'I can handle her.'

He pressed his lips to her forehead and lingered there. 'I have no doubt you can.' He trailed a light path down the slope of her nose, then fastened over her mouth in a gentle evocative kiss that stirred her emotions and sent them soaring high.

'Hmm,' she accorded lightly, minutes later. 'This is nice.'

He swept an arm beneath her knees and carried her to bed. 'It's about to get better.'

He'd kept his word, she aknowledged on the edge of sleep. And then some. With a long, slow loving that had touched her heart and reached right down to her soul.

CHAPTER ELEVEN

DINNER held in the ballroom of a city hotel, an entertaining speech by a prominent international author, followed by the launch of his latest book, promised to provide an interesting evening.

Doubly so, given a percentage of the ticket price comprised a donation to the author's favoured charity.

Gianna dressed with care, choosing an elegant evening gown in floral silk chiffon. Make-up was understated, with emphasis on her eyes, and she swept her hair into a casual twist and secured it with a jewelled comb. A diamond pendant, matching earstuds and bracelet completed the outfit, and she slid her feet into stilettos, caught up an evening purse and descended the stairs at Franco's side.

'Anamaria and Santo will be joining us. We'll collect Anamaria first, then Santo.'

Surprising, considering the grandparents had handed over nearly all evening social obligations more than a year ago.

'Tonight's guest of honour numbers high on a list of Anamaria's favourite authors.'

Anamaria *and* Santo...together? Oh, my, the evening had just gone from entertaining to *interesting*.

'Maybe we should seat them apart?' Gianna suggested as Franco sent the Mercedes down the driveway, and he shot her a musing look.

'You think it'll make any difference?'

It didn't, of course. Anamaria was at her imposing best, while Santo seemed determined to tease.

Gathered in the lobby adjacent the hotel ballroom it was barely noticeable, given the number of mingling guests. However, seated at their designated table it was something else.

'Wine, my dear?'

Anamaria threw her nemesis a haughty look. 'The wine steward will take care of it.'

'Can't see one in sight.'

'Don't be impatient.'

'You are bent on telling me how to behave, *vecchia*?'

'I don't know *why* you had to be here,' Anamaria offered grimly, and pursed her lips at his slightly wicked smile.

'To keep you on your toes.'

Gianna barely avoided rolling her eyes. It was going to be a doozy of a night!

She nudged Franco's thigh, and pleaded quietly, 'Do something.'

'What would you suggest?'

'A slap on each wrist?'

'Figuratively?' he said with mocking humour.

'Of course.'

'They'll quiet down soon.'

Now she did roll her eyes. 'Don't bet on it.'

There was a lull as Anamaria pointedly conducted what appeared to be a pleasant conversation with a neighbouring guest, and Santo, not to be outdone, turned to the guest seated next to him and did the same.

The wine steward tended to the wine, while the MC provided background information on the author, cited the nominated charity, then announced the first course would be served.

'About time,' Santo declared as a waiter delivered starters to their table.

'Incorrigible man,' Anamaria accused, *sotto voce*, and accompanied it with a look set to kill.

Santo merely smiled.

The main course duly followed, and they managed to get through it without further mishap.

'He's quite a character, isn't he?' a fellow guest murmured as a waiter began collecting china and flatware.

'Quite,' Gianna agreed, aware in private he was a very warm-hearted man. It was only in the company of Anamaria Castelli he became a teasing fiend who delighted in ruffling the older woman's feathers.

She cast an idle glance over the large ballroom, stilled suddenly as she caught sight of a familiar head, and wondered why she should be surprised to see Famke the centre of attention at a distant table, with yet another high-profile male as her partner.

To prove she could get anyone she wanted?

The MC appeared at the podium and began the lead-up to the guest author's appearance by listing his credits on the *New York Times* and international bestseller lists; then he gave the introduction.

Enthusiastic applause greeted the dapper middle-aged man who took the microphone with professional ease. Practised in the art of crowd-pleasing, he proceeded to do just that, with an amusing tale of his path to publication, fame and fortune.

Dessert was served, followed by coffee, and afterwards the book-signing was announced, whereupon guests began to form a queue in order to buy the book and have the author script a personal message.

Anamaria leaned forward. 'Shall we join them?'

The queue had become incredibly long. 'Why don't you stay here?' Gianna suggested. 'I'll organise a copy for you.'

'Thank you.'

She began threading her way through the many tables, and reached the end of the queue mere seconds ahead of Famke.

Coincidence, or a staged confrontation?

The latter, she cynically alluded beneath her breath. Had to be. And just what she needed to cap the evening!

'Famke,' Gianna acknowledged with marked civility.

'When are you going to get the message?' the actress demanded without preamble.

Why play pretend? 'Maybe you should ask yourself that question.'

The queue moved forward a few paces.

'There's a law against harassment and stalking,' Gianna continued quietly. 'Persist, and you'll find yourself in an invidious position.'

For a moment she thought Famke would strike her, and she mentally reeled at the degree of hate mirrored in the actress's eyes.

'Don't gamble on keeping Franco,' came the cool rejoinder. 'You'll lose.'

She was way past playing *polite*. 'With you continuing to lie?' She waited a beat. 'Did you think I wouldn't check?'

Gianna caught sight of Franco walking towards her, and she sent him a warning look. This was her fight, and she'd do it alone.

'We speak on the phone every day.'

'You send text messages…which Franco chooses to ignore.'

Famke gave a vicious smile. 'You can't be sure of that.'

'Yes,' she said carefully, 'I can.'

'I'm not done with you.'

'Give it up, Famke,' she advised quietly. 'Leave with your credibility and your reputation intact.'

'Go to hell.'

Gianna effected a slight shrug. 'Your choice.'

The actress gave her a withering look, then turned and walked back to her table.

Oh, my, that was fun.

Franco closed the distance between them, and she looked at him wordlessly.

'I take it Famke changed her mind about waiting in line?' Franco drawled as he threaded his fingers through her own, then brought them to his lips.

Warmth seeped into her body at his touch, and for a few timeless seconds her eyes locked with his.

Something was happening here, an intrinsic magic that had everything to do with the senses. And more. So much more. Almost as if their souls merged and became one.

Crazy.

Everything faded, and she became oblivious to the venue, the people, noise.

There was only the man.

Had she been so intent on examining her own feelings she hadn't seen what she'd perceived as the impossible?

Because she'd prepared herself so well to accept a convenient marriage, to accept affection in place of love...that she'd dismissed the possibility it might change?

Franco hadn't uttered the *love* word...but then neither had she.

Oh, Lord, was it fanciful thinking on her part, and she was seeing something that didn't exist?

The answer was simple...she could ask him.

Sure, a tiny voice derided. Just come right out with *Do you love me?*. That would go down well.

Even a one-second hesitation on his part, and she'd die.

A slight movement, the touch of his hand against the back of her waist, and she became aware of her surroundings.

'Not long now,' Franco indicated, and she realised they must have moved forward, for there were only about a dozen people standing in front of them.

Minutes later they bought the book, the author signed it, and they returned to their table.

'Thank you.' Anamaria opened the cover, read the inscription, and smiled. 'I shall treasure it.'

'That actress give you any trouble?'

Santo's questioning demand resulted in a faint smile.

'Nothing I couldn't handle,' Gianna assured quietly.

'Can't abide stupid women.' Santo turned towards Franco. 'Take care of it.'

'Already done.'

The drawled pitch in his voice feathered her spine.

Somehow she couldn't see Famke walking away without one last attempt at creating trouble. Delusion didn't factor in logic or reason, and unless she was mistaken the actress would push until she reached the limit.

Where and when that might occur would be difficult to predict.

'Are you ready to leave?'

The guest of honour stood encircled by a group of avid fans, and several people were drifting towards the exits.

Anamaria stood to her feet. 'If you don't mind?' She shot Santo a dark glance as he prepared to take her elbow. 'I'm not exactly decrepit.'

'Last time I heard, you complained of a sore ankle.'

She had? Gianna couldn't recall her grandmother mentioning any such injury.

'You're imagining things,' the older woman dismissed.

It was late when they finally reached home. It had been quite an evening, and Gianna ascended the stairs while he locked up and set the security alarm.

She felt unusually tired, and she slipped out of her stilettos when she reached the main bedroom and discarded her clothes.

Bed had never looked so good, or felt so comfortable, she decided minutes later as she slid in between the cool sheets.

When Franco entered the room she was already asleep, and he stood looking at her pale features in peaceful repose...the soft texture of her skin, the gentle fan her eyelashes formed as they lay closed over her eyes. The delicate curve of her mouth.

Her inviting kissable mouth, which he doubted he'd get to kiss any time soon.

She was something else, he mused as he shucked his clothes. Woman, witch, and the light of his life.

How could he so much as *look* at another woman when he had her?

Soon, very soon, they needed to talk.

But not tonight, he determined as he slid into bed.

He snapped off the bedside lamp, then settled close and gathered her in.

CHAPTER TWELVE

THIS ball numbered high as one of the major charity events of the year, with funds raised donated to aid a Leukaemia foundation.

Held in the ballroom of a major city hotel, the many guests included the wealthy, the society matrons and those who liked to appear to be *seen* attending every event on the city's social calendar.

An eclectic mix, Gianna observed as she entered the spacious lobby at Franco's side.

The men looked resplendent in black dinner suits, and there were designer gowns in abundance. Jewellery sparkled beneath the lights, and there was the buzz of conversation as guests caught up with friends, associates, while sipping champagne.

Judging by the attendance the night's goal for funds raised would be met. With several guests contributing large donations, the equipment needed would soon be in place.

Would Famke put in an appearance tonight?

A bubble of cynical laughter rose and died in her throat. *What are you thinking?* The chances of the actress missing an opportunity to put herself within Franco's radius were nil.

Yet, although it irked her, even brought her to anger, the deep-seated fear she'd harboured from the moment Famke appeared on the scene had begun to diminish.

There were too many inaccuracies in the actress's barbs. Franco could dispel them with unquestionable proof.

Mayhem didn't cover what Famke intended to cause. It went deeper than that as she systematically and very cleverly launched one attack after another.

Delusional psychosis?

The actress's behaviour was a worry, and verged close to requiring legal intervention.

Would Franco take that step?

'I doubt Famke will be here.'

Gianna glanced up at his powerful features, glimpsed the warmth apparent in those dark eyes, and felt a piercing sweetness flow through her body.

For a moment she could almost believe he cared...really cared. And she slipped a hand into his, felt the answering pressure, and watched his mouth curve into a generous smile.

'Want to bet?'

There were friends they needed to catch up with, polite exchanges with several acquaintances as the lobby became crowded with fellow guests.

'Love your gown.'

Gianna turned to find Nikki Wilson-Smythe within touching distance, and she returned the compliment. Nikki looked stunning...with the perfection it took most of the day to achieve.

'Estella has excelled herself.' It was true, for the colours emphasised Gianna's skin colouring, enhanced by make-up and the subtle shadings of eyeshadow and lipstick.

She'd adhered to Estella's advice and swept her hair into an elegant smooth twist, and worn the jewellery pieces suggested.

'The ballroom doors have just opened,' Franco advised. 'Perhaps we should take our seats?'

Their reserved table was well positioned, and within minutes the remaining eight seats were filled.

Gianna breathed an inward sigh of relief. If the actress did show this evening, she hadn't been able to manipulate the seating arrangements.

The MC gave an amusing introduction to the charity's president, who in turn lauded the tireless work of committee members, achievements,   goals,   and   projections.

Images shown via slide projection and video camera touched the hearts of many. Children, some very young, with large solemn eyes, a smile at simple pleasure, and laughter in spite of adversity.

There was entertainment carefully slotted in between each course, and the food was superb.

It was during the main course that Gianna experienced a vague prickling between her shoulderblades, and she moved her shoulders slightly in an attempt to ease it.

'Something wrong?'

She incurred Franco's swift gaze with equanimity. 'I'm fine.'

Except the feeling persisted, and she glanced around the room, witnessed nothing untoward and continued with her meal.

There was a break as waiters moved swiftly to clear the many tables, and it gave her the opportunity to turn slightly in her seat.

It was then she saw Famke, seated two
tables away, and for a few heart-stopping
seconds the breath caught in her throat at
the stark venom evident.

'You've seen her.'

How did he guess? 'You have eyes in the
back of your head?'

Did she know her pulse had picked up its
beat and visibly thudded at the base of her
throat? Or that her breathing changed when
she became mildly agitated?

He knew everything about her, *aware* and
attuned to her in a way he'd never experienced with another woman.

'Yes. Don't visit the powder room alone.'

'You plan on causing a riot by coming
with me?'

His fingers tightened over her own. 'Ac-
companying and waiting for you.'

'My own personal bodyguard,' Gianna
alluded with a touch of musing cynicism.

'Minimising any opportunity Famke
might seek to upset you.'

Well, there you go. 'Protection, huh?'

'That bothers you?'

'Not in the least.'

The MC took the podium and announced another round of entertainment, after which dessert and coffee were served.

It was then Gianna excused herself and rose to her feet. 'There's no need—' She left the rest of the sentence hanging as Franco followed her actions.

Was Famke watching?

Without a doubt.

It sickened her to think the actress was willing to go to extraordinary lengths to cause trouble.

When would she give up?

The line in the powder room was quite long, and it was a while before she emerged to join Franco and resume their seats.

She didn't spare a glance in the direction of Famke's table, and now the meal was concluded, so too the evening's entertainment, it was pleasant to converse with the guests sharing their table.

'Bart wants to spend the rest of his days on board ship,' his wife confided. 'Can you imagine?'

'Restrictive, perhaps?' Gianna suggested, aware Franco appeared deep in conversation with the woman's husband.

'Sweetie, no. We'd live permanently on board and travel the world. With the option to stay anywhere we chose, then fly to rejoin the ship.'

Ah, *that* ship. Touted to be the world's largest floating hotel, with luxury suites re-sembling small apartments.

The society doyenne would have a ball…literally.

'I'm sure you'll love it,' she endorsed warmly. 'Think of the fun, the shopping. And the social life must be incredible.'

'Hmm, perhaps you have a point. We *do* have family scattered all around the globe.'

'Dinner with the Captain, the senior staff. The people you'll meet.' She was getting carried away here. 'The privileges. The food.' Maybe she was in the wrong business! 'Entertaining.'

'Keep talking.'

'Permanent duty-free shopping?'

'Uh-huh.'

'No cooking or cleaning? No need to fight traffic or find parking?'

'I'll tell Bart to pull out all those brochures again. This could be a very good thing.' She patted Gianna's hand. 'Thank you, my dear.'

'You should be in marketing,' a male voice suggested with quiet amusement, and she turned to the attractive young man seated opposite.

An irrepressible smile curved her lips. 'I am.'

'Perhaps I should head-hunt you.'

'With an offer I can't refuse?'

It was light-hearted fun, for he knew exactly who she was, and to whom she was married.

He named a figure that was so far over the top it was ridiculous, and wrought an appropriate response.

'You're a comedian.' Laughter emerged as a sultry chuckle. 'Your CEO would throw an apoplectic fit.'

'Ah, but then I am the CEO.'

'Really?' She wasn't quite sure she should believe him.

'Really.'

'Well, now there's the thing. Franco has no option but to afford me a higher salary package.'

'Failing which, you *will* join my company?'

He couldn't be serious, surely?

'No,' Franco intruded smoothly, 'she won't.'

'Pity. She's quite something.'

'Yes, she is.'

Mine. The word remained unspoken, but the implication was crystal clear.

Wow. She felt quite...bemused. Franco acting the proprietorial husband was an unaccustomed role.

The waiters circulated the tables, offering more tea and coffee, which Gianna refused.

The MC took the opportunity to thank the guests, the hotel venue, and then proceeded to announce the amount raised by the evening function.

Several of the older guests began to drift towards the exits, while staff efficiently reorganised sufficient floor space to enable those choosing to dance.

The band assembled, the music began, and couples gradually took to the floor.

It seemed natural to take Franco's hand and join them.

She'd danced with him countless times, and being held in his arms wasn't a new experience. Except there was some ephemeral magic heightening the existent sensuality and taking it to a place where it was all too easy to imagine they were one being. Twin halves of a soul.

It made her want to wind her arms around his neck and pull his mouth down to hers. To take and possess. Without reservation or inhibition.

This close, she was aware of the strong substance of his arousal, could feel the beat of his heart and sense the slight muskiness of his skin beneath the civil sheathing of clothes.

Humans in an animal kingdom…or vice versa? Each prey to the emotional and physical needs of the flesh.

'Home?'

There was a slight huskiness in his voice, and she shifted a little, easing out of his arms as he led her back to their table.

It took only minutes to bid goodnight to those remaining seated, and considerably longer to clear the ballroom and arrange for the concierge to have the Mercedes brought to the hotel entrance.

It had been a pleasant evening, and she said so, enjoying the silence as the car whispered through the broad streets.

'It's not over yet.'

She turned towards him. 'Promises, huh?'

Lovely. Every minute of it. From the time they ascended the stairs and entered the bedroom.

Franco removing the jewelled clip from her hair, letting its length fall free.

The sensuously slow peeling off of each layer of clothes, followed by a leisurely loving that lasted long through the night and continued into the early dawn hours.

Perfect.

CHAPTER THIRTEEN

THE third morning in succession, Gianna pondered when she felt...*different*.

It wasn't anything she could pin down, just a subtle change. A slight increase in appetite, a mild aversion to some of her favourite foods, and her breasts seemed more...sensitive.

Maybe something she'd eaten? And she'd developed a tendency towards tiredness after dinner, was ready for bed earlier than usual, and falling asleep almost as soon as her head hit the pillow.

Then realisation began to dawn...

No, it couldn't be.

She did the maths, counting back...and sank into a nearby chair as she absorbed the possibility.

A whole gamut of emotions swirled through her body...excitement, anticipation, joy. And a smidgen of concern.

A baby?

The need to *know* brought her to her feet, and she collected her shoulder-bag, caught up her keys and headed the BMW towards the nearest pharmacy.

There was a tendency to purchase the pregnancy test and rush home. Except she forced herself to wait, and spent time visiting one of the city's Sunday markets, browsing the stalls, checking out crafts and pottery, needlework.

She bought a few things, one of which would serve as a gift for Rosa, paused long enough to sip a cool drink, then retraced her steps to the car and drove home.

Franco appeared for dinner, then disappeared into his study to check his notes. Meetings on the Gold Coast were scheduled for the next day, and there was a need to plan his strategy.

Gianna delayed going upstairs on the pretext of selecting a book, one of several she'd been recommended to read.

Do the test.

OK, so she'd read the instructions and think long and hard about it.

Idiot.

Oh, for heaven's sake. *Just do it.*

It came up positive.

A pleasurable glow suffused her body, and she hugged her arms together over her midriff. Well, isn't that something?

First up in the morning, she'd make an appointment and have her doctor complete an official test.

Meantime, she'd keep the news to herself.

It was easier than she thought, for she didn't stir when Franco came to bed, and when she woke in the morning he'd already left for the airport.

Gianna managed to snare an appointment at three that afternoon, and the day seemed inordinately long as she dealt with phone calls, made several, and participated in a three-way conference call with executives in Brisbane and Sydney.

There was a half-hour delay at the medical centre, but she emerged with the knowledge she was seven weeks pregnant.

It seemed incredibly *real*, this tiny foetus, and she was sure her feet didn't touch the ground during her walk to the car.

A baby.

Gianna's mouth curved into a winsome smile as she took the elevator up to the high floor housing the offices of Giancarlo-Castelli.

She wanted to call Franco, but he was tied up in meetings and wouldn't be home until late, and she needed to share it in person, not over the phone.

It was almost six when she finally made it home.

There were a few messages, and she showered, changed, then fixed herself a mushroom omelette, added salad, and followed it with fresh fruit.

She was keying notes into the laptop when her cellphone buzzed with an incoming message, and she read the text with a sense of mounting anger.

Famke, bent on creating mischief and mayhem.

Don't wait up. We're on late flight.

Gianna's eyebrows rose. *We?*

Dammit! The chances of Famke being with Franco were slim. Discovering his movements wouldn't be difficult, given the blonde's resourcefulness combined with a total lack of scruples.

Logic provided realistic answers. Yet it was the *illogical* Gianna had a problem with!

Oh, get over it!

She knew where he was at any given time…didn't she? He made sure she was aware of his schedule. He rang in if he was going to be late. It was a courtesy they each observed.

Except there were gaps. Slices of time he could easily manoeuvre to his advantage...if he chose to.

Don't go there. You have no need to.

It was useless to wish Famke to another planet. Another country would be ideal! Hell, she'd even settle for another city!

Yet the actress was determined to create mischief and mayhem in Melbourne.

Worse, she was adept in covering her tracks.

Franco didn't appear to buy into it. In fact, Gianna was almost willing to swear he found Famke's persistence just as tiresome as she did.

At that moment her cellphone rang, and she activated it automatically.

'Dinner took longer than expected,' Franco offered. 'I'm taking a later flight.'

Gianna's fingers tightened on the slim flip-top 'So don't wait up?' Her voice was cool, cooler than she'd intended.

'The delay is unavoidable.' His voice was a silken drawl.

'Of course.'

'I'm about to take a cab to the airport. I'll see you when I get in.'

'I'll be asleep.'

'In that case, I'll wake you.'

He disconnected the call before she could answer, and she issued a heap of pent-up ire on his unsuspecting head, only to retract most of it minutes later.

She attempted to continue working, only to give it up after half an hour. For a while she surfed the television channels, then she closed it down, collected a book and settled herself in bed.

When she discovered she was re-reading pages and skipping others entirely she consigned the book to the bedside pedestal and turned off the lamp.

Sleep came easily, with the hormonal weariness of early pregnancy. At some stage she sensed Franco's presence, felt his body warmth as he gathered her in, and luxuriated in the brush of his lips to her temple, her cheek, before her mouth.

The inclination to murmur a token protest became lost as his hands skimmed beneath her oversize tee-shirt and sought delicate curves, exploring sensitive hollows with a touch that brought her *alive* and aching.

Oh, dear heaven… She wanted, needed to hold on and never let go.

'Shh,' Franco murmured as he removed the tee-shirt and buried his lips into the curve at the base of her neck. 'Let me do all the work, hmm?'

He did, with a gentle thoroughness that brought forth a shimmer of tears. The acute sensual awareness he aroused was almost too much, and the breath hitched in her throat as he savoured each pleasure pulse until she begged for his possession, exulting in the magic they shared.

Passion, at its zenith, with the power to liqueify her bones.

Together they reached the heights, held on, and lost themselves in mesmeric sensation so exquisite she wanted to capture it and never let it go.

Good sex, she acknowledged on the edge of sleep. Better than *good*, and was aware it was more, so much *more*.

They should talk. And they would. Tomorrow.

Except she woke late, discovered she was alone in the bed, and a glance at the time sent her racing for the shower.

Franco was shrugging into his suit jacket when she entered the kitchen, and she crossed to his side, cupped his face and brought it down to her own.

'What's your schedule for today?'

He deepened the kiss, and took it to a place where she had to catch her breath.

'Are you suggesting we play truant?'

His drawled query brought forth a rueful smile. As if!

'Lunch,' Gianna capitulated.

Did she imagine his brief speculative appraisal? 'One o'clock?' He named an up-market restaurant within a short walking distance from their city office building. 'I'll book a table.' He reached the door. 'I have a late morning appointment across town. I'll meet you there.'

'OK.'

She had muesli and fruit for breakfast, followed it with hot sweet tea, then drove into the city.

The morning proved uneventful, for there were no panic calls, no dramas requiring her immediate attention, and at ten to one she freshened her make-up, caught up her shoulder-bag and took the elevator down to street level.

It was a lovely day, the sun high in a cloudless sky, and she stepped onto the pavement with a light heart.

Lunch with her husband. A secret smile curved her lips. A child. Theirs. Boy or girl? She had no preference, only that it was born healthy. Names? Was it too soon to give names a thought?

A nursery? A bedroom close to their own. For a minute or two she thought colour schemes, a nursery mural... It was like discovering a new world. She entered the restaurant, spoke to the *maître d'*, then followed in his wake.

She saw Franco, and was about to lift a hand in greeting when she glimpsed a familiar blonde being seated by a uniformed waiter.

'Ah,' the *maître d'* relayed, 'your friend has arrived.'

Friend? You have to be kidding!

The temptation to turn and walk right out again occurred as a momentary thought. Except as a solution it sucked.

Franco, to give him credit, appeared to be dealing with a mixture of surprise, dismay...and as she drew level his facial features assembled into a hard mask.

Famke, on the other hand, acted the shocked mistress caught out to perfection. *'Gianna.'*

Oh, my, she was good.

'We didn't expect to see you.'

How could the actress have known *which* restaurant, the time...unless she was bent on deliberately checking every restaurant booking within a walking radius of Giancarlo-Castelli?

Gianna suppressed a faint shiver, and speared Famke's guileless blue gaze.

'Really?' She injected cynicism into her voice. 'I find that strange, given Franco and I made arrangements to meet here.'

She shifted her attention to Franco, and her eyes hardened in silent warning as he appeared to speak.

This was her game. She was the one in control.

'What will it take for you to butt out?'

Famke gave a tinkling laugh. 'Perhaps you should ask yourself that question.'

'I already know the answer.' Hell, she hoped she did! 'I'll make it easy for you.'

This had to stop, and stop *now*. If it involved a public display...then so be it.

'I'm going to walk out of here. Franco can follow or stay.' She waited a beat. 'His decision.'

She was oblivious to the silence, the veiled interest of fellow patrons. What was more, she didn't really care!

Nor did she spare him so much as a glance as she turned and threaded her way towards the entrance. The *maître d'*, the waiters, suddenly became galvanised into action, and there was the clatter of flatware on china, the chink of goblets as patrons returned their attention to the meal.

She wouldn't look back. Instead, she inclined her head to the *maître d'* as she passed the front desk, and kept on walking.

Gianna reached the pavement and automatically turned and began retracing her steps to the office. On a subliminal level she registered how her mind seemed separate from her body…she was walking, weaving her way through the lunchtime men and women crowding the pavement, but she didn't *see* any of them.

'You were quite something back there.'

Her heart seemed to stop, then kick-start into a faster beat at the sound of Franco's voice.

'Go away.'

'Not in this lifetime.'

Her stomach executed a crazy somersault. 'I'm not in the mood for small-talk.'

'Small-talk isn't what I have in mind.' He took out his cellphone and keyed in a number on speed-dial. 'Reschedule all my afternoon appointments for next week.' He paused fractionally. 'Notify my wife's PA with an identical instruction.'

Gianna looked at him in consternation. 'You can't do that.'

Franco slanted an eyebrow, then keyed in another digit on speed-dial.

It was the first of several…arranging for Enrico to collect Gianna's car…notifying Rosa they'd be away for a few days.

They reached the entrance to their office building, summoned the elevator and took it down to the underground car park.

Seconds later the doors slid open.

Disbelief was etched on her features. 'You can't just walk out.'

He fastened his mouth on hers for a brief moment, then released her. 'Watch me.'

He led her towards his Mercedes and unlocked the passenger door. 'Get in.'

Stunned, she complied without argument. Home in the middle of a week-day afternoon didn't sit well, and she was about to say so when she noticed they weren't heading towards Toorak.

'Where are we going?'

'To a hotel.'

'Excuse me?'

Franco spared her a brief musing glance. 'You heard.'

'Why?' The query sounded impossibly childish even to her own ears, and his husky chuckle was almost her undoing.

Minutes later he swept the Mercedes into the entrance of one of Melbourne's most luxurious hotels, handed the keys to the concierge, and dealt with check-in.

'What do you mean, we're staying here a few days?' Gianna demanded as they took the elevator to a high floor.

'No interruptions, no intrusions.'

'But we don't have so much as a change of clothes!'

The elevator slid to a halt and they exited the cubicle. 'So we purchase whatever we need.' He checked the numerical directions and led her to their designated suite.

The carded access provided entry, and she uttered a startled gasp as he swept an arm beneath her knees and carried her inside.

'Are you mad? Put me down.'

He did, but he didn't let her go, and Gianna looked at him wordlessly as he slid his hands up to cup her face.

'Franco—'

'Shut up,' he bade gently as he lowered his head down to hers.

His mouth was incredibly gentle, and he sensed the faint trembling of her lips as he brushed them softly with his own.

She was so petite, yet so strong. Vivacious in a way that lit up his world.

'Do you have any idea what you do to me?'

She wasn't sure she could even *think* as he teased open her mouth and deepened the kiss into something that made her lose all sense of time and place.

'You're wearing too many clothes.'

His soft laugh feathered down her spine. 'Let's take this slow, *cara*. Hungry?'

'Are you talking food or sex?'

'Both.'

'I get to choose which comes first?'

He was here, with her, which had to mean something. His belief in the sanctity of marriage? A deep-seated sense of duty?

Oh, dear heaven...something more than affection? She hardly dared hope it could be *love*.

'We're going to talk,' Franco voiced gently. 'Make love. And eat.' He traced the curve of her mouth, lingered a little, then drew her in, so close she couldn't help but be aware of his arousal. 'Not necessarily in that order.'

Sensation spiralled through her body, meshing with heat and need.

She'd come this far, weathered much...and she wanted for it to be right.

An impish smile curved her lips and lent a sparkle to her eyes. 'Food.'

He wanted to laugh, and almost did. 'Witch.'

Gianna crossed to the courtesy table, selected the Room Service menu, picked up the phone and placed an order.

Franco extracted his cellphone, set it to the message bank, and suggested she do the same.

'Incommunicado?'

'Is that such a sin?'

For a man who was so business-oriented, accessible at any time of the day or night either by cellphone or e-mail, it was quite a departure.

She looked at him carefully, noting the well-defined facial bone structure, the slight groove slashing each cheek and the fine lines fanning from his eyes.

She bore his name. She was pregnant with his child.

He had her heart, her love, unequivocally and without question.

'No,' she managed calmly. 'Just... unusual.'

'Impossible I might choose to make you the sole focus of my attention?'

A sharp rap on the door announced the waiter's arrival, and minutes later Gianna began doing justice to a delicious Caesar salad.

Franco's prawn risotto looked tempting, and she had no hesitation in sampling a proffered offering.

There were questions she wanted to ask, but they seemed difficult to voice, and she felt as if she were teetering on the edge of a precipice...unsure whether she'd maintain her balance or fall off the edge.

A panoramic view of the Yarra River and tall city buildings of steel, concrete and glass in varying architectural design stood against the skyline. Trees, their wide-spreading branches heavy with green foliage. Traffic building up at intersections.

'Are you done?'

Gianna viewed the small amount of salad remaining in the bowl, aware she couldn't eat another mouthful. 'Thanks.'

Franco stacked the tray and deposited it outside their suite.

If there'd been luggage she could have unpacked…except that wasn't an option. She rose to her feet and endeavoured to conjure up something to do.

'Don't.'

She shot him a startled glance and lifted an involuntary hand, only to let it fall as he crossed to her side.

'Look at me.' He caught hold of her chin and tilted it, then cupped her face between his hands and brushed a thumb-pad along her lower lip before fastening his mouth on hers in a kiss so incredibly gentle it brought the sheen of unshed tears to her eyes.

'What does that feel like?'

Someone who cares. 'Good,' she acknowledged, and glimpsed his faint smile.

'And this?' His mouth took possession of hers, and it became more, so much *more*.

She lifted her hands and linked them at his nape, drew him close and held him there as she savoured the intimacy, the heat, the passion...and, unable to help herself, she answered it with her own.

A tiny seed of hope took root and began to grow as he lifted his head and slanted an eyebrow in silent query.

Gianna offered a witching smile. 'One of your better efforts.'

'With room for improvement?'

A teasing verbal dance...she could do that. 'On a scale of one to five, I'll award a score of three.'

Liar. He achieved top score every time.

His soft laughter curled round her nerve-ends and pulled a little. 'Minx,' he accorded lightly.

There was never going to be a better time, and her amusement faded. 'Famke.'

Franco didn't pretend to misunderstand. 'Taking the first available flight to London.'

The blonde actress had finally got the message? 'Really?'

His eyes momentarily hardened. 'The threat of a stalking charge proved a convincing factor.' His hands slid beneath her breasts and lingered there, soothing the full curves, each sensitive peak.

'I see,' Gianna managed quietly.

'Do you?'

Did he have any idea how emotionally fragile she felt?

'You decided not to upset the status quo.'

He wanted to shake her, and almost did. 'Fool.'

Franco searched her expression, caught the latent tremulousness beneath the surface of her control, and sought to demolish it.

'A long time ago Famke occupied a few months of my life,' he stressed gently. 'She wanted a commitment I wasn't prepared to give.' He paused fractionally. 'Not then. Not ever.'

His eyes seared her own, and she couldn't look away.

'You were determined to see what she wanted you to see.'

'She was very convincing.'

A muscle bunched at the edge of his jaw. 'Indeed.' He lifted a hand and brushed gentle fingers across her cheek, then let them rest at the edge of her mouth. 'She's not *you*,' he said quietly.

The *hope* plant grew an inch. She couldn't say a word, dared not, and his smile assumed a warmth that came close to melting her bones.

'Do you seriously think I put a ring on your finger out of *duty*?'

'I was given that impression.'

'Not by me.'

Her eyes widened. 'Anamaria—'

He pressed a finger over her mouth. 'Conspired with Santo. And succeeded. Only because *love* was part of the equation.' He caught the sheen of unshed tears, and pressed his lips to each eyelid in turn.

'Fool,' he reiterated gently. 'How could you not know?'

'You never mentioned love.' If he had, she'd have gifted him her soul, along with her heart.

'I thought I did…with my body as I worshipped yours. Each kiss, every touch.'

She wanted to weep, and struggled to keep her emotions intact. 'You do the sex thing very well.'

The edge of his mouth lifted in humour. 'Is that so?' His lips touched hers, nibbled a little, then rendered a punishing nip.

Gianna responded in kind, sensed his indrawn breath, and couldn't resist teasing him. 'Maybe we can work on it a little.'

'I plan to. Soon.' He held her at arm's length, and the look in those dark eyes made her catch her breath. 'But first…the words, hmm?'

The air seemed trapped in her lungs, making it difficult to breathe.

'You're the light of my life. My love…everything,' he vowed quietly. 'For as long as I live.'

Somewhere in her mind the *hope* plant burst through into the sunlight and embraced new life.

'Same goes.' The breath hitched in her throat. 'No one comes close.'

She needed to show him just how much he meant to her, and she lifted a hand to cup his cheek, felt the press of his lips as he caressed her palm, and felt her bones liqueify.

Gianna reached for the buttons on his shirt and dealt with them, suppressing the desire to rush. They had time…all the time in the world…and she wanted to share something infinitely slow. A mutual supplication of the senses. *Lovemaking.*

Almost as if he *knew*, he began dispensing with each layer of clothes until none remained, and Gianna stood still as he took in her slender curves.

'You're beautiful,' Franco accorded gently.

A lump rose in her throat, and she swallowed it down.

'In your heart, your soul,' he added. 'Where it counts.'

'I think you'd better stop with the words right now.' Her voice choked. 'Or I'm going to cry.'

'*Cara*—' He glimpsed the evidence of tears. 'Don't.'

With one hand he dispensed with the bed-covers, and drew her down with him onto the fresh bedlinen.

His hands skimmed her silken skin, soothing, arousing as he created havoc with each and every sensual hollow, then followed the path with his mouth.

She became lost, swept into a sea of passion where there was only the two of them. Skin on skin as they rose together, scaled the heights, urging each other on until they merged body and soul.

It was a while before they rose from the bed and showered. Towelling guest robes hung in the wardrobe, and they pulled them on, then stood together at the window, watching the lights spring on over the cityscape as dusk descended, together with multicolored flashing neon signs.

The Yarra River became a wide dark grey ribbon, and the traffic from this height resembled cars in miniature.

Franco's arms curved her in close against him. 'Do you want to eat in, or go out?'

'In,' Gianna said without hesitation, and felt the slight pressure of his chin as he rested it on top of her head.

They conferred over the menu, ordered, and when the food was delivered they fed each other morsels, then settled back replete.

It didn't seem fair to keep the news to herself any longer.

'How do you feel about parenthood?'

Franco leaned back in his chair and his eyes acquired a quizzical gleam. 'In general, or in particular?'

For a moment she didn't answer, and she saw his eyes sharpen.

'Are you trying to tell me something?'

'I'm pregnant.' So much for setting the stage! Just blurt it out, why don't you?

He sat forward in one fluid movement, and she rushed on before he had a chance to say a word. 'Seven weeks. It was confirmed yesterday.'

His features were a study of concern and joy.

Gianna focused on the joy. 'I planned to tell you over lunch.'

A man so in control of his emotions, she doubted anyone had seen him so vulnerable.

It made her feel...empowered, as only a woman could be. Sure of her love, the man in her life, and sharing the special gift of the child—God willing—she'd bring into the world around seven months from now.

Franco crossed round the table and hunkered down at her side. 'Are you OK with it?'

She touched a hand to his cheek, and felt her heart turn over when he covered it with his own. 'Are you?'

'You need to ask?'

A smile curved her generous mouth. 'I take it that's a *yes*?'

'Without question.'

A light laugh bubbled from her throat. 'The grandparents are going to have a field day.' She rolled her eyes expressively at the thought. 'Can we keep the news to ourselves for a while?'

'Anamaria is sharp as a tack. You think she won't pick up on you declining wine with a meal?'

'Probably not.'

He leaned in and kissed her...long and slow, with incredible gentleness. 'Let's celebrate.'

'I thought we'd decided to stay in?'

Franco rose to his feet and lifted her into his arms. 'We are.' He crossed to the bed, propped up the pillows with one hand, then settled down with her on his lap.

'I need to hold you. Be with you.'

'Oh. That kind of celebration,' she teased.

'Love you. All the days of my life.'

'Not the nights?'

'Those, too.'

Gianna reached up and traced the outline of his jaw. 'You're going to be a very busy man.'

He caught hold of her hand and pressed it to his lips. 'Count on it.'

EPILOGUE

GIANNA GIANCARLO gave birth to twins via Caesarean section seven months later. A boy and a girl, possessed of their mother's eyes and dark hair.

Named Samuel and Ann-Marie, they were the light of their parents' lives.

The christening proved to be a joyous event, with family and close friends present to witness the blessing of two infinitely precious children, after which a celebratory lunch was held at Franco and Gianna's home.

Shannay cradled Ann-Marie, who cooed and smiled, and kicked her little legs in delight at all the attention.

'She's beautiful. And so content.'

Franco curved an arm around his wife's shoulders. 'Like her mother.'

Gianna looked up with a smile that touched his heart. 'While Samuel is very much his father's son.'

Right on cue Samuel cried, and Anamaria scooped him from Santo's arms with a glare in silent accusation.

'They need to be fed and put to sleep.'

'The child told you that?'

'What would you know?'

'They're at it again.' Gianna felt the brush of Franco's lips against her temple. 'I'll go rescue the infants and tend to them.' She offered Shannay a smile. 'Want to come with me?'

'Thought you'd never ask.'

Gianna took Samuel, and together they ascended the stairs to the nursery.

Murals in pastel colours decorated the walls, attractive mobiles hang suspended high above each cot, and stuffed toys of varying size sat bunched on every surface.

'Wow, I'm impressed.'

Gianna settled in a comfortable rocking chair and began nursing her son.

'I hope I manage as well when I have mine.'

She shot Shannay a piercing look. 'Is that a general comment, or…?'

'Three months.' Shannay's smile lit up her features. 'Apart from family, you're the first to know.'

'Hey,' she said gently. 'That's wonder-ful.'

'Tom thinks so, too.'

'And Tom's children?'

'There's the thing…they're delighted— dreaming up names, suggesting which room will be best for the nursery. And Tom's mother is over the moon at the thought of another grandchild. So it's all good.'

Shannay hadn't had an easy transition as stepmother.

'I'm glad.' She disengaged Samuel and held him out to Shannay. 'Want to try your hand at getting him to burp while I feed Ann-Marie?'

It was later, when both babes had been changed and were settling sleepily in each cot, that Gianna had a chance to give Shannay a congratulatory hug.

'Who'd have thought a year ago we'd each be embracing motherhood?'

'It's lovely to see you so happy.'

'Thanks.' It's lovely to *be* happy. No need to pretend, or adopt a façade. No insecurities or doubts.

'Famke created a maelstrom.'

'Oh, yeah, and then some.'

Gianna adjusted the baby monitor, then caught hold of Shannay's hand. 'Let's go join the party, shall we?'

Franco crossed to Gianna's side as she re-entered the lounge. 'They've settled OK?'

'You've had the entire house wired so their slightest sound can be heard in every room,' she teased. 'If they cry, we'll know about it.'

There was much laughter and convivial pleasure as gifts were exchanged, gorgeous outfits in pink and blue added to an already extensive collection of baby clothes.

Anamaria presented each child with documentation for a sizable trust fund, which Santo generously matched.

It was late afternoon when the last guest departed, with the exception of the grandparents, who were invited to stay on for dinner.

A meal that survived without opposing banter from Anamaria or Santo. Something which surprised their grandchildren and drew speculative interest as the evening progressed.

Anamaria, who never added alcohol to her coffee, suggested a nip of brandy would do very well—which, given the champagne toasts, and wine with dinner, put her over the limit to drive.

'Perhaps you should consider staying in one of the guest rooms?' Gianna suggested.

'Rubbish,' Santo refuted. 'I'll drive her home.'

Anamaria lifted an eyebrow in imperious query. 'In the Ferrari?'

'You have a problem with that?'

Gianna glimpsed the silent challenge, and wondered at it.

'Grazie.'

You're joking…aren't you?

'Well, what do you know?' Gianna said quietly, as Santo saw Anamaria seated, then climbed behind the wheel and sent the gleaming red Ferrari purring down the driveway. 'My grandmother hates that car.'

'Does she?'

Gianna gave him a perceptive look. 'You think…?'

'They have a thing going?' Franco closed the door and set the security alarm. 'Do you?'

Did she? Maybe. 'I'm trying to get a handle on the possibility.'

A plaintive cry sounded as they crossed the lobby, and was followed by another when they ascended the stairs.

'Right on time.'

They entered the nursery together, and Franco lifted his daughter and deftly effected a diaper change while Gianna tended to her son.

She glanced at the man cradling their daughter, and her eyes misted at the sight of them. The babe so infinitely precious, the man equally so.

'Thank you,' Franco said gently. 'For being the love of my life. The gift of our children. The world as I know it.'

'Right back at you.' She felt tears gather, and blinked them away.

Her son finished feeding, and she nursed Ann-Marie while Franco took care of burping Samuel.

Both babes settled with barely a murmur, and Gianna checked the monitor, dimmed the lights down low, then quietly followed Franco from the room.

In one fluid movement he swept Gianna off her feet and carried her to their bedroom.

'My turn, I think.'

She'd seen the need in those dark eyes, and the love.

It overwhelmed her, as it always did, to know she alone possessed the power to enchant and delight him.

'I love you so much,' Gianna said quietly as he drew her in and began to show her, as only he could, just how much she meant to him.

Love beyond doubt. Unconditional and everlasting.

Two kilometres distant, Santo Giancarlo assisted Anamaria Castelli to her front door, unlocked it and watched her step inside. Then she turned towards him, head held high, and solemnly thanked him for the ride.

'There's just one thing.' She paused. 'Next time you take me out in that car, perhaps you can open it up a bit? I understand it's built for speed.'

'It's Italian,' he said solemnly.

'So,' came the dignified reply, 'am I.' And she closed the door on him.

Who'd have thought?

Santo almost laughed out loud as he swung in behind the wheel, and there was no one to see the teasing smile curving his mouth.

Life, he decided, was about to become even more interesting.

MILLS & BOON® PUBLISH EIGHT LARGE PRINT TITLES A MONTH. THESE ARE THE EIGHT TITLES FOR JUNE 2006

———— ❦ ————

THE HIGH-SOCIETY WIFE
Helen Bianchin

THE VIRGIN'S SEDUCTION
Anne Mather

TRADED TO THE SHEIKH
Emma Darcy

THE ITALIAN'S PREGNANT MISTRESS
Cathy Williams

FATHER BY CHOICE
Rebecca Winters

PRINCESS OF CONVENIENCE
Marion Lennox

A HUSBAND TO BELONG TO
Susan Fox

HAVING THE BOSS'S BABIES
Barbara Hannay

MILLS & BOON®

Live the emotion

0506 R

MILLS & BOON® PUBLISH EIGHT LARGE PRINT TITLES A MONTH. THESE ARE THE EIGHT TITLES FOR JULY 2006

❦

THE ITALIAN DUKE'S WIFE
Penny Jordan

SHACKLED BY DIAMONDS
Julia James

BOUGHT BY HER HUSBAND
Sharon Kendrick

THE ROYAL MARRIAGE
Fiona Hood-Stewart

THE WEDDING ARRANGEMENT
Lucy Gordon

HIS INHERITED WIFE
Barbara McMahon

MARRIAGE REUNITED
Jessica Hart

O'REILLY'S BRIDE
Trish Wylie

MILLS & BOON®

Live the emotion

0606 Rom LP